AF506729

Mother of Pearl

A SAPPHIC SUGAR BABY ROMANCE

A. A. FAIRVIEW

Copyright © 2024 by A. A. Fairview

Cover illustration by Sophie Zuckerman

All rights reserved.

No part of this book may be reproduced in any form or by any electronic or mechanical means, including information storage and retrieval systems, without written permission from the author, except for the use of brief quotations in a book review.

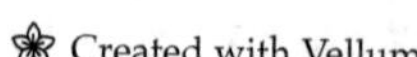 Created with Vellum

Contents

a Note on Content   1
Chapter 1   3
Chapter 2   15
Chapter 3   22
Chapter 4   33
Chapter 5   46
Chapter 6   67
Chapter 7   86
Chapter 8   100
Chapter 9   107
Chapter 10   118
Chapter 11   130
Chapter 12   138
Chapter 13   152
Chapter 14   167
Chapter 15   177
Epilogue   184

Acknowledgments   189
About the Author   191

a Note on Content

THIS IS A SAPPHIC MONSTER ROMANCE.

It features an age gap relationship, tentacles, and sexually explicit content involving fish eggs.

There is also alcohol consumption and discussions of infidelity not involving the main couple.

CHAPTER

One

A FAINT BUZZING WAKES ME, the bathroom lights a halo in the water. I sit up in the bathtub, the familiar splash comforting. I climb out of the tub and shut off the alarm on my phone. A message pops up reminding me today is my first day lifeguarding at the country club.

With my phone no longer screaming at me to wake up I run my slick hands across my deep blue scales, droplets of water flicking off and falling to the tile below. I spread my hands and shake them out, water splashing off the webbing between my fingers. When people hear Fishfolk the first thing they picture is mermaids, with their thick heads of hair and eyes that lure you in. Even I'm not immune to a mermaid's gaze.

I'm nowhere near as distracting to sailors. I've got legs, two of them if we're being specific. My body is very Human, though my hips and chest don't have the curves of a Human woman. My scales appear in patches along my body, most of them on my collar and tops of my thighs. Across my ribs are gills though they're not all that noticeable outside of the water.

As I comb my blonde hair with my fingers, there's a knock at the door.

Jessie shouts, "I gotta pee! Please Lydia!"

I roll my eyes before opening the door for my Human roommate who blushes when she sees me naked. I snort, leaning against the doorframe. "See something ya like?"

She blinks. "Yeah." Then points to the toilet.

I step out of the bathroom and let her have her turn. All my clothes are stored in her room anyway. Dressed, I walk past the balcony where Goldie stretches in her nest, the sunlight catching her feathers that shine as bright as her name.

Goldie and Jessie have been friends since middle school. They needed a third roommate for their apartment and I needed a place to live while working the summer at The Serpent's Oasis, a country club in Northern New Jersey. Previously I'd worked at an indoor saltwater wave pool just outside the city where bougie Humans and monsters alike would go to get pampered at the fully decked out spa.

Unfortunately, my ex works there— and has been there longer. Some breakups involve kids or pets, mine involved my cushy summer lifeguard gig.

Anyway, I figured Jessie would be chill since she was already rooming with a monster girl. *Super* chill when I did a little internet sleuthing and found old Goldie also likes women. When I asked if I could claim the bathroom as my bedroom, she said yes without any questions. I could sleep in a bed but I'd wake up so dehydrated and no one wants that. Plus it would make the whole place smell like dried fish.

Goldie steps out from the balcony, "Happy first day!" she sings.

"Thanks," I yawn, giving the coffee maker more attention than my roommate. Goldie munches away on granola.

Jessie is the last to join us. "I drained the bathtub, I hope that's okay."

I nod, still not having it in me to be cordial without caffeine. The coffee maker beeps and I grab three mugs from the cupboard.

"None for me," Goldie squawks. "Caffeine makes me sick."

I nod, still learning the ins and outs of Harpies. Everyone is different on a biological level. I need to stay moist, Goldie needs to be able to make a nest, and Jessie, well, from the way she gulps down her hot coffee, needs caffeine more than me.

"So, excited for your first day at–" She takes a dramatic breath. "–Serpent's Oasis?"

"Sure." I shrug. "Looking forward to schmoozing with rich people."

I'm not kidding. My business major at NYU will only take me so far— I need connections. A fancy-ass country club in the lake district of New Jersey is the perfect place.

Jessie rolls her eyes. "At least you're ready for that. Schmoozing and flirting are the same thing right? Because lots of married men are going to flirt with you."

"If it gets me an internship at a fortune five hundred, I might even bat my eyelashes and tell them 'oh how interesting' when they brag about their golf strokes."

Goldie chirps, "And when they're interested in other strokes?" She makes a crude gesture with a clawed hand.

Jessie lightly smacks her friend's wing. "Don't scare her! The old men are annoying but they're not perverts. Promise."

I shrug. I have bigger gripes with rich people, like their inability to follow directions or take no for an answer. They're more like toddlers than frat boys going on about how hot they find lesbian porn. "I'm sure I'll survive."

———

THE SUMMER HAS JUST BEGUN and already Jessie's car smells like sunscreen. As we pull into the country club I get my first good look at the place, a three story tall mansion with a nice view of one of the many man-made-lakes in this part of the state. The club itself doesn't boast that the lake isn't natural, but a pretty quick internet search will tell you most of the lakes in this part of the state were made by rich yuppies trying to escape the hustle and bustle of the city.

Internet's words, not mine.

Jessie parks her car in the employee lot hidden behind a tall topiary wall. We pull up next to a parked car still occupied by its driver. The engine is off with the guy just sitting in the front seat head back like the ceiling of his car is so interesting. Jessie snickers before honking her horn. The man jumps and I realize I know him. Carl, one of the club managers, looks at us with one angry eye. I've only spoken to him over video call before now and sheepishly waved at him.

Carl groans as we all get out of our cars. He's shorter than I imagined him. I guess it's hard to separate Cyclops from the myths that surround them. He's far from a three story tall hulking sheep eater. I don't even think he's taller than six feet. He's just lanky.

"Ready for a summer of fun!" Jessie chirps like the most obnoxious pep rally leader possible.

Carl ignores her and plants his eye right on me. "You're Lydia, right?" He offers his hand and I give it a shake.

"Nice to meet you Carl. Thanks for the job."

He snorts. "Yeah, let's see how long you feel that way. Come on, I'll bring you to Lord Unnith and we can get you onboarded."

I'm never one to forego research so I know Unnith is the Dragonfolk who owns The Serpent's Oasis. But a Lord? I'm pretty sure owning land in Northern New Jersey doesn't make someone a Lord in the legal sense. Dragonfolk do love their titles. Almost as much as they love their treasure hoards.

I give Jessie a wave before following Carl inside the club. The floors are all polished dark lumber while the walls are a crisp white, reflecting the light off the chandeliers that feel wholly unnecessary with such low ceilings. Carl guides me forward as we pass old photographs and commemorative plaques. Before we turn down a hallway I notice an already occupied indoor bar.

Carl knocks at a door labeled Oasis Manager but doesn't bother for a response before opening the door. A gush of hot air hits me before I see a big red Dragonfolk sitting at a desk. He grins, showing off an intimidating set of teeth. "Carl! Just the man I was looking for. You finished that bartending training right?"

"I still think selling alcohol poolside is a bad idea."

Bold move, certainly not one I would make but Unnith must trust Carl to keep the peace.

Unnith blows smoke out his nose as he laughs. "Too late! Already stocked the shack. Dragon's Red Tonics are a go!"

Too afraid to find out what a Dragon's Tonic is or if it comes in multiple colors, I step past Carl to introduce myself. "Hi, Lord Unnith? My name is Lydia, I'm one of the lifeguards this season." I wait to see if he offers to shake my hand.

"I'm sure you are Lydia." He looks at Carl. "Does she need anything?"

Carl shrugs. "Direct deposit paperwork and her uniform. Otherwise, everything else she *should* have finished online before coming here."

I pull out some paperwork, online certificates confirming I know how to perform CPR, water rescues, and first aid. In theory. None of my certificates have lapsed so the online stuff was just a refresher. It's so strange tapping a mouse to do chest compressions.

Lord Unnith takes the stack of papers and flips through them, before setting them on his desk. As he signs each one, he congratulates me. "Welcome to the team!"

———

I CLAW at the nylon clinging to my ass, trying and failing to get my swimsuit to cover me. The country club provides all lifeguards with swimsuits, which seemed like a good deal till now. One tentacle tip pokes out and I reach to slip it back in. The bundle of tentacles strains against the fabric making it appear like I'm smuggling something between my thighs. When I worked at the wave pool, the dress code was more lax, myself and other Fishfolk opting to wear swim trunks— not swimsuits with bottoms like g-strings.

Rolling my eyes I accept I'll need to tuck. There's waterproof tape, I just don't have any right now. So instead I cup my tentacles and try to wrangle them, shoving them back and keeping my legs tight. Watching myself in the mirror, it works for a solid second before they start to writhe and make themselves known again.

Fuck it— I'm not here to pick up women. And even if I was, they would sort of have to be into my little bushel of fun.

I walk to the lifeguard stand to relieve Jessie who almost looks asleep, her chin in her hand and a big pair of sunglasses hiding half her face, her whistle hanging loose around her wrist. "Hey," I call up and she turns to look at me. At least I think she's looking at me past those dark brown shades. "We're switching. Anything I need to know?"

One hand points to a pack of three boys, one sitting on the pool's edge and kicking his feet to splash his two other friends who are swimming around him. "I've had to warn them not to dive in the deep end twice."

"Are they strong swimmers?"

"I'd hope so if they're trying to dive in a seven foot deep pool." With that she hops off the chair and hands me the radio. "Good luck, I'm on lake duty next."

I nod and climb up to sit on the raised wood chair. It looks like the kind of stand you'd see at a beach but the country club is a few hours drive from any proper ocean. The lake next to the country club has plenty of pond scum but it's nothing compared to seaweed. I know Humans get the ick from that stuff but chlorine is much worse. I'm biased— the stuff dries my scales and checking the levels every few hours is a pain.

Slipping on my aviators I do a scan. Three boys playing in the deep end with who I presume is one of their dads sitting on his phone in the shade. An elderly woman does a lethargic breaststroke. It's pretty dead. I spot Carl, with his forearms on the counter of the Grub Shack, looking as bored as I feel. His single eye opens and closes slowly. It's hypnotic and I have to look away.

I twirl my whistle around my finger to keep myself occupied while the sun beats down on my neck. The pool gate opens and a little girl in a pink floral swimsuit comes bounding in. "Walk!" I shout, maybe a bit preemptively but better safe than sued. She stops in her tracks before walking forward. A boy, maybe a year or two older than the girl, has matching swim trunks and rash guard, a pair of goggles on his head. Behind them both is a woman in a black swimsuit, a large sunhat and glasses hides her profile.

Her body is fucking fantastic though.

Wide hips and thighs, big breasts, the tops spilling out from her swimsuit. She adjusts her hat and I see she's got perfectly manicured bubblegum pink nails. It almost clashes with the rest of her conventional outfit, but it's the only thing that really differentiates her from the dozen other rich moms that I've seen poolside.

She settles in one of the beach chairs and takes off her sun hat. Her hair is black, same as her swimsuit, with gray roots and some gray flyaways at her temple. I glance back at her kids and notice they're both young and blond. Grandkids? Maybe she's the nanny? I guess women have kids older and older nowadays, especially wealthy ones. Got to secure a spot in the corporate hierarchy before going on maternity leave.

My thumb trails across my bottom lip as I keep eyeing her, wishing she would take off her sunglasses so I can get a better look at her face. There are some smile lines around her lips but otherwise her skin looks smooth and well cared for. If I wasn't on the job I would ask her what sunscreen she uses.

The sound of thrashing and splashing pulls my attention away from the woman. The three boys from before are now just two as they shove their friend under the water. I blow my whistle, the distraction enough to get their hands off the kid and he surfaces. "That's your third warning!"

"No it's not!" One of the kids wines.

"We're just seeing who can hold our breath the longest."

The dad is still on his phone. Typical.

"Hold-your-breath games are not allowed at the pool. And this *is* your third warning."

I glare at the dad, not that he's looking or could tell past my sunglasses. *Get off your fucking phone and collect your damn kids.*

The little boy with the goggles hops into the pool. My eyes dart back and forth between him and the other boys. The kid floats up but his face is still in the water and his feet are off the ground. Most people would just think it's a kid having a little fun but I know he might be stuck, unable to right himself.

I stand up, grabbing the rescue tube when there's another splash. The woman in the black bathing suit is wading her way through the water towards her kid. I still hop into the water to assist. She gets there before me and lifts him up, the kid gasping for air. The mom looks at me with a frown and pleading eyes, her dark brows furrowed.

"Here." I put the rescue tube under his arms and gently take him from her, then start pulling him towards the shallow end with the steps. He kicks his feet like the tube is a boogie board. At least he's not upset.

He sits on the steps and I ask him some questions while checking him out, making sure his lips aren't blue or he isn't dazed in any way. His mom stands nearby, holding herself. "I'm *so* sorry," she says. "He's been taking swim lessons, I thought he would be alright without one of those floaty things but I guess not."

"Hey, it happens." I hear the three boys from before snickering in the deep end of the pool. "At least you were paying attention," I say loud enough for the entire pool to hear. "Not every parent does." I glare at the dad still tapping away at his phone.

She reaches over and rubs her son's back. "What do you say?"

"Thanks!" he says. I notice he's missing one of his front teeth.

I offer him a soft smile. "Let me get you a swim vest."

I go and grab one from the bin and bring it over, snapping him in. Then I run my fingers along the float around his chest making sure it's not too loose or too tight.

"Can I go swim now?"

This kid has no idea he almost drowned. "Sure, go ahead."

He starts running.

The mom and I both shout. "No running!"

We look at each other.

"I'm so–"

"You apologize a lot."

She blinks and I bite the inside of my cheek. Was I rude? Will she complain to Carl? Or even worse— Lord Unnith.

Thankfully, she chuckles and pushes a strand of silver behind her ear. "Can I have your name? Let the managers know you're doing a good job."

I'll give you my number too– I think but don't dare say. That will definitely get me in hot water with Lord Unnith. Heck, maybe even Carl who I swear is watching me with that single, dark brown eye. "It's Lydia."

"Pretty." She extends a hand and I look for a wedding ring. "My name is Stephanie." I shake her ringless hand.

The little girl in the pink swimsuit comes over and hugs Stephanie's leg. "Mommy, I want ice cream."

Stephanie sighs, "Sophie sweetie, you can't go swimming if you have ice cream."

"Yeah," I back her up, "Causes cramps. Real bad."

Stephanie gives me a closed-lip smile.

I'd love to try and chat her up, figure her out. But there are three boys in the deep end I have to deal with and a deadbeat dad I've got to judge. Hopefully, Stephanie's glowing review will offset whatever bitching results from me actually doing my job.

The next hour is uneventful. The three boys behave. The old lady finishes up her lethargic laps and settles on a chair to dry in the sun. Stephanie watches her kids, resting her head and her hand and smiling like her son's little splashes are the most darling thing in the world. Eventually, her daughter leaves the little kitty pool and settles on her chest, looking like she might fall asleep. Stephanie strokes her daughter's hair and gives her a little kiss on her crown. It's so stinkin' adorable.

When her daughter returns to the kitty pool, Stephanie stretches out on the deck chair. Her lips part, a phantom moan filling my ears. Water droplets sparkle along her thick, soft thighs. I have to cross my legs to make sure my tentacles don't go haywire.

———

THE SMELL of chlorine now lingers in Jessie's car and I already miss the sunscreen. I rub my scales, the film of chemicals giving me the ick. "You think I can request to just be put on lake duty?"

Jessie shrugs. "Probably. I know some lifeguards are freaked out by how dark the water gets. How do you feel about inner tubes?"

I raise a brow. "Neutral? Why, are they a pain?"

"Kids using them as trampolines is annoying. Grown men who make more money than I ever will smacking each other with them is why I talk to a therapist once a week. Besides, the hot moms always hang out by the pool." Jessie takes her eyes off the road to smile at me, looks forward, then looks back at me.

"Can you please focus on the turnpike?"

Jessie does but there is a sly smile on her face. "You made a face like you knew exactly who I was talking about."

"No I didn't." I lie— Stephanie is still fresh in my mind. I'm sure there will be plenty of other hot moms cropping up this summer. There were plenty at the wave pool too, but Stephanie is nice. It turns out *nice* does something to me. Her curves help, the charming gray streaks in her hair…

"What's her name?" Jessie asks.

"Eyes on the road," I scold. "Besides, hot moms usually have husbands. I'm not trying to be a homewrecker."

We make it back to the apartment without another mention of moms or work. "Dibs on the bathroom," I announce as I step into the tile.

Jessie groans. "Ugh fine. Just means I can take as long as I'd like later."

Fine by me. I just can't stand the chlorine on my scales. In the bathroom I completely turn the hot water knobs and grab a vitamin C tablet. The bathroom closet is packed with all my amenities; seaweed bath bombs, phosphate and vitamin tablets, and an assortment of oils. It's not cheap. Everything specially formulated to keep the water at a safe PH. Not all of it is necessary. Hot water alone would clean me fine but why not add a little something to take the edge off my first day?

As I strip out of my clothes I run my hands along my gills stretching across my ribcage. They're tense, not having much room to breathe in that tight swimsuit. I wonder how long I have to work at Serpent's Oasis before I can ask for a uniform change. I'd be much happier in swim trunks and a sports bra.

Once the bath is full and steaming I slip into the water. My gills flex and it's like breathing fresh air for the first time all day. I guess the one good thing about the one piece is it helps prevent any chlorine from getting in my gills. They would filter out all the bullshit but it's sort of like knocking back shots of everclear and just letting your kidney do all the heavy lifting.

I disappear beneath the water, holding onto my knees in an attempt to float. My eyes are designed to see under the water but I close them, thinking about today… About Stephanie… her heavy breasts and round hips. How soft her lips might feel against my scales.

I sit up in the water, my tentacles waving in the water, opening up like a flower. It's been *a while* since I've been touched. I don't mind but my body has a different opinion.

I clap my hands around my cheeks like waking up from a bad dream. Except a dream about Stephanie wouldn't be so bad… With a washcloth I clean off my scales then drain the bathtub. It's the shortest bath I think I've ever taken.

CHAPTER
Two

STEPHANIE and her kids are pool regulars, showing up every day like clockwork at eleven. Her son wears floaties in the water while her daughter just sits at the pool's edge and watches. Sometimes she brings dolls and dips them in the kiddie pool to play mermaids. It would be nice to just sit and watch Stephanie tan all day but I know I'll get lost in her curves and someone will drown.

And fuck me, these rich folks *love* to almost drown.

You'd think rich people would pay for swim lessons but nope. Some of these people own boats for God's sake.

Maybe it's not completely their fault. Lord Unnith's Dragon Red Tonics and four dollar beers can't help things. One of those plus the hot sun and I'm stuck pulling middle aged men out of the water.

"Sir." I paddle towards a guy I watched knock back four cold ones in the last hour. "Would you like assistance?" His head is barely above water, his hands flapping just under the surface but doing little to keep him afloat.

A bit of pool water spills into his mouth. "I'm fine!" He gurgles.

I keep treading water, waiting for the moment his head

inevitably slips beneath the water. Which sounds messed up but it's not my fault we're not allowed to save people without their consent. Its reverse rules: consent is implied when someone is passed out in the water.

"Logan!" I look over and see Stephanie standing at the pool's edge, her arms crossed over her chest. A few other people have gathered and a kid stands on the pool ladder, watching. "Just accept the help, you're embarrassing the whole country club."

Logan spits out water. "Fine!"

I passed him the rescue tube. "Grab–" He grabs it with his arms and legs. Luckily this thing is designed with brainless behavior in mind and he floats fine. I drag him to the shallow end and get him on dry land to check him out. He reeks of beer. Carl agrees to cut him off before leaving to fetch a cup of water. I advise Logan to sit in the shade for at least an hour.

I'm about to climb back up onto the lifeguard stand when I hear a familiar voice. "Right back to work, huh?"

I look over my shoulder at Stephanie, giving me that closed mouth smile that's deadly charming. I don't know how she's single. If she is single that is. No ring I've seen, and all the ladies here have big-ass rocks on their fingers. But maybe she doesn't want it getting damaged by chlorine or lose it in the pool filter.

My own words haunt me, *most hot moms have husbands.*

I fail to say anything clever. "Yup." I hop up and settle back into my seat, welcoming the hot sun as it dries my body.

"What do you do in the winter?"

That I do have a clever comeback. "I lifeguard those polar bear plunges." I shoot her a wink before putting my sunglasses back on. "I'm a student. Getting my degree in business."

She tilts her head. "Well this is the perfect place to work. Great networking opportunity."

"Somehow I doubt Logan over there will want to hire me

after I just dragged him out of the pool and put him in time out." I look over to see Logan pouting while a towel around his shoulders. Big toddler.

"You don't want to work for him anyway," she tells me. "Terrible at logistics. Never meets deadlines."

I slide my sunglasses down my nose, peaking over the lenses though I'm still facing forward watching the pool. "And you know this because…"

"I do market analysis. I know more about everyone here than even the most gossipy of wine moms."

So she knows all the haves and have-nots. God she's so hot. And there are have-nots here. It's people that spend the most have the least liquid cash while the frugal types are the ones raking it in. I saw it first hand at the salt water pool, families who would come one summer then gone the next. Meanwhile the folks who only did spa treatments when there was a sale came back every summer.

My eyes linger on the artificial blue of the pool. "So… You know all the dirt."

"Dirt, no. I don't know anything shady. Technically everything I know is public information. I just bother to actually keep track."

"Unlike Logan."

"Right. Seeing as he can't keep track of how many beers he's had in an hour…"

I snort, wishing I could ask her to stick around for my thirty minute break. Even if she did, her kids are still with her, both of them playing in the kiddie pool. Nothing says romance like sipping wine spritzers with two kids next to you munching on chicken nuggets.

As if she can sense my struggle, Stephanie says "I'll get out of your hair."

I ignore my job to watch her walk away, the curve of her ass poking out of her swimsuit. It would be kind of nice if she caught me staring.

"Oh," she stops and adrenaline starts to pump through my body, fearing and hoping at the same time that she's about to call me out. "If you ever need help with an internship... Can I give you my number?"

"Sure," I croak.

Stephanie goes to her bag, bending at the hip as she rummages around for something. The curves of her ass meeting her thighs is a perfect, plump heart. As she walks back I remind myself this number is for business, not for pleasure.

She hands me a business card and I slip it in my fanny pack without really looking at it. "Thanks Stephanie."

"You can call me Steph." With that she walks to the shallow side of the pool to gather her son.

"What was that?" Carl has water with a lemon slice in his hand.

He's managed to spark the excitement built up in my body and I jump. "Th-the drowning?" I say in-between breaths. "Or... what?"

He points at my fanny pack. "I heard her offer you her number and you slipped something in your bag."

I chose my next words carefully. Lord Unnith might be the owner but I get the impression Carl is the boss. "She wanted to know what I do for work, told her I'm studying business, she offered to help me with internships."

The truth is easy but my gills still flex like I've told a lie. For the first time I'm grateful for the one piece suit.

"No schmoozing on company time." With that he leaves to bring Logan his drink.

What kind of rule is that? There's no way he doesn't sense that something else is going on, but it doesn't matter when it's all one-sided. If it is one-sided...

———

Hi Stephanie, it's Lydia. Just wanted to
confirm this is your number. Thanks for
offering to help me make connections.

Lydia hi! And please just call me Steph.

Oh it's no problem! I had plenty of women
help me when I was your age, good to pay
things forward.

Glad to hear you have that mindset. People
can be so cut throat in my degree.

I know what you mean. Can I ask why you
aren't doing an internship right now? (I'm
happy you aren't I'd much rather see you
every day)

I miscalculated and thought I was a shoo-in
for this one internship so I didn't really look
anywhere else. Didn't end up getting it.
Lesson learned.

Oh I'm so sorry. Hopefully they didn't string
you along.

It's fine! Like you said, it's much nicer seeing
you every day.

Plus can't beat the sunshine every day.

I'm sure you'd rather not be babysitting
drunk adults by large bodies of water.

The pool is small compared to the wave pool
I worked previously. But you're not wrong.

As nice as the sunshine is, just let me know
when you start looking for an internship and I
can connect you with some folks.

I appreciate it, Stephanie, really

*Steph

;)

————

WATER LAPS at my elbows as I stare at that winky face emoji. I couldn't wait when I got home to text her. So while I sat in my bath with a seaweed bath bomb I sent her a cordial text. Rereading our texts I try to pinpoint who flirted first, if this *is* flirting. Stephanie– Steph, is nice, genuinely so so nice, maybe that's all this is.

I set my phone down and try to ignore the butterflies fluttering about my stomach.

My tentacles dance in the water, waving at me, mocking me as the warm butterflies in my gut fly further south. I bite my lip. Jessie is waiting for her turn in the bathroom, we've already fallen into a routine. She might notice if I spend more time in the bath…

Fuck. I haven't been able to get Stephanie out of my head since we first met. Opening my legs my fingers push aside my tentacles, my clit already throbbing. Rubbing little circles across it, my head rolls back in the water. The warm water to die for between my legs.

With my other hand I slip a finger inside my cunt, pretending it belongs to Stephanie, imagining her cuddled up behind me with her lips pressed against my ear. *You're so beautiful… Please fuck me next…*

I whimper and tip my head forward in the water so little bubbles escape my mouth instead.

I have no idea what Stephanie is into but in my fantasy, she loves my tentacles, loves my thick clit and wants it in her mouth, wants me to *breed* her. More bubbles surround my face as I rub faster and faster. *Good girl… That's it— spill for me.*

The first egg pops out of my clit, the size of my thumb tip.

My tentacles get to work, grabbing it and releasing it into the water. Ideally, it would deposit the eggs inside my lover. Fill her completely with my eggs till she spills, nothing more than a breeding farm. It's going to be a mess cleaning this up but I couldn't care less as a second egg spills from inside me, making my thighs shake. I take my clit between two fingers and carefully tug at my bud, milking the eggs from inside me.

Meanwhile I slip another finger inside me. *Such a greedy cunt.* A third finger inside me, curling my fingers to press against my g-spot. I gasp, warm salty water filling my mouth. What I would give to suck on Stephanie's heaving breasts. To make her moan with my mouth. More and more eggs pop out of my clit and I imagine my tentacles pushing them inside Stephanie, filling her better than her husband, better than any fucking man.

I imagine her trying to close her legs while my tentacles tease her clit, while they shove my eggs inside her... stroking her hair while I suck on her breasts and neck... Whispering that she's such a good mommy to my little eggs.

More and more I spawn in the bathtub, my eggs floating to the water's surface. *Such a dirty girl... My little pervert making a mess of herself.* "Fuck—" I choke, my pussy tight around my fingers as the last batch of eggs pours from my clit, my tentacles grabbing each with fervor. Still riding out my orgasm I keep my fingers inside me, scissoring them and considering touching myself more— rubbing my clit raw till it hurts to walk.

Then I remember my roommates. That I have a spawn of eggs to clean up. I could let them circle the drain but it might cause problems with the plumbing. Last thing I want is to explain to our landlord why our bathtub is clogged. I huff, bubbles erupting around my face.

CHAPTER

Three

WALKING up to the pool to relieve Jessie, I spot Stephanie sitting at the pool's edge with her feet in the water. Her kids are both wearing floaties and splashing about. I try to focus on that and not the fact she's wearing a bikini. Up until now she's only ever worn one piece suits, all of them nice and tight, clinging to the round, firm body– driving me crazy.

Now I can see the edges of her heavy breasts, a thin string connecting the two triangles of fabric which by some miracle keeps her covered. White streaks, much like the silver strands of her hair, run up along her stomach. I'd love to run my tongue over them, call her mommy while she rides my fingers. Or my face.

I'm biting my lip when she waves at me. She smiles, this time showing off her pearly whites, the wrinkles around her eyes and cheeks more apparent. The smile she's given me up till now was demure and mysterious. This smile is adorable and it makes me smile right back.

I forget about Jessie and go to Stephanie "You look nice."

She looks down at her body and I wonder if she sees what I see. "It's been a while…"

"I would never have guessed." I'm not about to tell her

she looks sexy or that she should wear less more often. One, she always looks sexy and two, I'd rather drown in seven lousy feet of water than tell a woman what to do.

Okay, if I've got my tongue inside her I might get a little bossy but that's neither here nor there.

Stephanie has her hand resting on her collar and I notice her nails are perfect after a week of daily pool use. "Do you always go pink?" I point at her nails. "They're pretty."

"You noticed?" She holds out her hand, fingernails catching sun rays. "I hate whenever the color chips. Much easier fix when I stick to the same color."

"Which is?" I know she has the exact brand and shade number memorized. She just seems the type. Reliable and distinct.

"It's—"

"Steph!" a gruff voice shouts. We both turn to see a man marching toward us. "What's the deal? It's my weekend with the kids."

Her voice is calm in stark contrast to his tone. "I thought you said you were going up to the cabin with some friends?"

This guy looks closer to my age than Stephanie's. Blond, built– has trophy husband vibes. If he weren't redder than a lobster dinner, I'd say good for her.

"They canceled. So it's my weekend. Come on you two!" He calls to the kids who look at him wide eyed and confused.

I can't keep my question to myself. "Do they even have their stuff?"

His head shoots in my direction like he's a dog who's just noticed another dog near his property. "Who the hell are you?"

I point at the lifeguard symbol across my chest.

"Roman, she's right. All I've got is a change of clothes in the car for after they're done swimming. All their weekend stuff is at home."

"Well pack them up and we'll go back to your place and get their things."

"I'd rather not spend that much time with you," she replies.

Roman scoffs. I purse my lips to hide my amusement.

Stephanie stands up. "I'll get their stuff out of the car and you can drive over and get their things. Spare key is where it always is."

"Thank you for being *reasonable*."

I wonder, since I'm off duty, how bad it would be if I shoved him into the pool. I don't even think he's a country club member, so really I'm just being the bouncer. But I resist, giving Stephanie a sympathetic look before leaving to relieve Jessie.

She climbs down from the stand since no one else is in the pool. "He seems charming," she mutters with a nod toward Roman.

"He had to be at some point right? Why else would you have kids with someone?"

Jessie pushes her sunglasses up to her forehead. "I think it has less to do what's inside his chest and more to do..." She circles the air around his torso with her finger.

I get it on an aesthetic level. It's not like I do crunches because they're fun. But I still don't get why Stephanie would bother with his attitude. Besides keeping things cordial for her kids...

"Guess being a lesbian has its perks." Jessie bumps me with her hip.

"Hasn't Goldie told you? Girls are even worse," I mutter before climbing up the stand.

The pool is empty. I tap my fingers on my chin, hoping someone will show up. I get my wish. Stephanie returns and for the first time ever, I see her get in, diving under the water and gliding along the bottom of the pool.

She surfaces and I feel like I'm watching porn. At least the first five minutes of it– the only actual good part where the pretty women are all dressed up in skimpy outfits, giggling and fondling each other. Once their clothes come off its crap. A bunch of contorted bodies, sharp nails, and fake orgasms.

But Stephanie, running her fingers through her dark hair while water droplets drip down between her breasts, is beyond sexy. Beautiful. Ethereal, even. She's real: gray streaks, stretch marks, wrinkles– the whole god damn package.

And finally she catches me staring. Even with my sunglasses she can probably tell, seeing herself in their amber reflection. My fingers are still on my chin and I let them drift up to my lips, my pointer finger rests on one corner while my middle finger rests on the other. I poke my tongue out then lap at the air like I'm licking at an ice cream cone.

Stephanie blinks. She backs up against the pool wall across from the lifeguard stand. Her arms reach up above her head, stretching, her breasts lifting as she takes a deep breath. The triangles of fabric fail to cover the undersides of her breasts, barely able to support them. Her hands rest on the back of her neck a moment before running down her collar. Bubblegum pink fingernails trace along her breasts. One of her fingers hooks around the string keeping those tiny slivers of fabric together and tugs at it.

I'm leaning forward in the stand now, as if that will offer me a better look. She releases the string with a snap, her breasts bouncing. We're so obviously flirting and I pray Carl isn't watching us. I jump off the lifeguard stand and grab the sign that says *Pool Closed*. As I walk away I feel Stephanie's eyes follow me. I tack up the sign before walking back to her with my hands on my hips. "Pools closed," I tilt my head. "Going to have to find some other way to entertain yourself."

"Oh?" she breathes, her bottom lip pouting. "I guess I should change then..." She pushes herself up out of the pool.

I look at the Grub Shack trying to catch a glimpse of Carl.

He must be doing stock in the back or something because he's not at the window. Stephanie starts walking towards the changing rooms, her wet bottoms clinging to her ass and I'm so tempted to grab at it. We're finally alone. No one would notice.

But I keep my cool, following her to the closed off changing rooms that are nicer than every public bathroom I've ever been in. Just before she enters the changing room she looks back at me. She smiles so wide I can see the tip of her tongue trace along her top teeth.

I lock the door behind us, the click of the tumblers like a switch in my brain. In an instant I'm holding her face and kissing those lips that have smiled at me for the past two weeks, making me wetter than Stephanie's swimsuit bottoms.

She whimpers, so desperate it drives me wild. Dying to hear her voice, I pull away, still holding her cheeks in my hands. "What do you like?"

"What?" she breathes. Her eyes are half open like she's waking from a dream.

I giggle, "What do you like? Oral, fingering... Do you want me to pull your hair?"

Stephanie's voice is still so breathy like my kiss pulled every ounce of oxygen from her lungs. "I've never done this before..." She admits and I see her cheeks are the same pink as her fingernails. "I... I've never been with a woman. Only Human men." Her fingers trace the scales across my collar. "I trust you, Lydia."

"I like when you say my name," I whisper before I lean in for another kiss.

Her tongue dives into my mouth and I let her have her fun while I tug the string behind her neck holding up her bikini top. It's like pulling on a bow atop the world's best birthday present. Her top falls and my hands take its place, cupping and caressing her breasts. They're heavy and hang low but I've never understood the obsession with perky tits.

These are much more fun to massage, more to grab, my fingers slide along her still wet body.

I release her lips and lean down to take a nipple in my mouth, sucking on it. There's a taste of chlorine but I don't care. I'll get to taste her properly soon, if she lets me. Stephanie's breath hitches in her throat and I glance up at her. She's looking down at me, her mouth agape. I pinch her other nipple between my thumb and forefinger and she yelps, before biting her lip and smiling.

My teeth gingerly tease her nipple and she hums. I can feel her chest vibrate against my lips, against my fingers. Fuck, tits are so nice.

I pull my mouth from her breast with a pop. "God, I'm obsessed with your body."

"R-really?"

"You didn't notice me staring at you like a horny teenager?" I keep pawing at her chest. "I've been ogling you since I started here."

"Maybe I did notice…" she admits. "But I told myself I was imagining things."

I straighten to kiss her again, lightly this time, while my hand trails down her stomach. "What else have you been imagining?" I ask, hoping to learn more about her fantasies. I have plenty, but my number one is making her finish so hard she forgets about Roman, forgets we're fucking in a changing room, forgets everything except me and my body.

Steph's hands finally start to explore, going straight for my ass. "I just wanted to touch you here." Her nails dig into my flesh.

"Really? That's all?"

"I'm not very creative," she admits. "Every time you'd climb up into the chair I'd check you out." She snaps the elastic of my swimsuit and a squeak of surprise leaves my lips. She pulls the fabric taut so my cheeks are out completely, then her fingers skim the round of my ass.

"God, whoever designed this must have been a huge pervert."

"Lucky for you."

Once she's done playing with my ass she grabs the straps of my swimsuit and pulls them down. My tentacles shift between my thighs, eager for her. I angle my hips so she won't feel them, but her hip snaps to mine like a magnet. "Oh you're so cute." She tells me, her hips grinding against my tentacles. They start to escape my swimsuit, latching onto her thighs. I run my fingers through her hair appreciating those gray streaks I've been admiring. She whimpers as I feel myself suction to her soft skin. "I want you," she breathes.

When I pull away there's faint popping sounds like bubble wrap, my tentacles are forced to release her. I take off the rest of my swimsuit. She does the same tugging off her bottoms. I get down on my knees where I have a full view of the hickey-like spots I've left around her thighs. As I admire them I touch the inside of her ankle, kiss her knee as my hand runs up the inside of her calf, then her thigh.

While my fingers run up her legs my lips find her hips, kissing those silvery stretch marks. Finally my hand reaches her crotch, her bush black and thick like the hair atop her head. I keep brushing my fingers along the very top of her inner thigh. "Can you open your legs for me?"

Stephanie does so and as soon as I have an opening, I grab her knee and hoist it over my shoulder. Stephanie gasps as her back hits the wall. Her folds are glistening, not with water but with her own wetness that I've been dying to taste. Sick of waiting, my tongue runs from the bottom of her cunt up to her clit.

Stephanie sounds like a soprano singing with vibrato. My tongue swirls around her clit, making sure to get her all worked up before finally wrapping my lips around it and giving it a light suck. "Oh fuck," her hands are deep in my hair, completely destroying my ponytail. "Don't stop," she begs.

So of course I stop to look up at her with a cheeky grin. Her bottom lip quivers. "Lydia," she whines."

"I'm sorry, mommy…" I watch her eyes trying to gauge her reaction to the pet name.

It goes better than I could have dreamed.

"You need to be good for mommy." She runs her hand down my cheek and holds my chin. "Follow directions for me, like a good girl."

So much for being the bossy part of this pair. I melt for her. "Yes, mommy." I take her clit back into my mouth, lapping at it like it's made of sugar and honey.

Stephanie rolls her head back against the wall, moaning *"yes"* over and over. *"God* yes!" I rub my thighs together for some relief– but it's not enough and I spread my legs wide, pushing aside my tentacles so I can bury my fingers in my cunt.

"You like this?" Stephanie breathes. She grabs the back of my head and shoves my head deeper between her thighs. "You like watching mommy? Fingering yourself like a big girl?"

I whine against her clit. It's impossible to decide what I like more, Stephanie all flustered and shivering under my touch or her in charge and grabbing me like I'm her favorite toy in her bedside drawer.

I start sucking harder, feeling her thighs shake. I bury my fingers inside myself up to the knuckle, curling my fingers as my cunt tightens around my digits. Stephanie pulls at my hair as she cries out, her thighs tight around my face.

Warm slick floods my chin. Stephanie relaxes, catching her breath. I rest my cheek against her thigh and look up at her flushed face as I continue to pump my fingers. Stephanie notices and coos, "Do you need mommy's help?"

I swallow. "Yes…"

"Yes what, dear?"

"Yes mommy, I need your fingers– or your mouth." It's my turn to sound desperate, my voice shaking. "Anything, *please.*"

"Stand up."

I do as she says, my legs shaking and my hand still pressed against my crotch. Stephanie takes my wrist and brings my hand to her lips, kissing my wrist before taking my fingers in her mouth and sucking on them.

I sigh, "And you say you're not creative…"

She smiles, my fingers still in her mouth.

Holding my wrist she pulls my hand back, her lips wrapping around my fingers as she drags them out of her mouth. She takes a step toward me, pinning me against the wall. Her fingers brush along my thighs. I open up my legs just enough for her hand to slip between them. My tentacles wrap around her wrist and I'm careful, not wanting to mark her skin there. We're teetering on obvious already.

Her lips find my neck as her fingers brush along my folds. "So eager for me."

Two fingers push up inside me and curl, pushing against my g-spot. I gasp involuntarily. Even if it's Stephanie's first time with a woman I'm not surprised she knows how to please me with her fingers. She *is* divorced, I'm sure she'd gotten a lot of solo practice since signing those papers.

She kisses my neck as her fingers work my cunt. "Fuck–" I curse as her fingers start moving faster. Her thumb brushes over my clit oh so slowly, especially compared to her fingers inside me. I managed to use my words, "Th-thank you, mommy."

She giggles against my skin. "Anything for my good girl."

She kisses down my neck and starts sucking at my collarbone. I wince and whimper. I'm afraid she'll leave a visible mark–or maybe excited by the prospect. The other country club moms judging me as I walk past–jealous of what they don't have. None of their husbands fuck me like Stephanie can.

My tentacles are now completely wrapped around her wrist, helping guide her, caressing her. Stephanie's thumb rubs circles against my clit and my cunt tightens around her fingers. "You look so cute when you're about to cum." She whispers against my skin.

I have to push my entire weight against the wall to stay upright as my legs shake. My heart races and I throw my head back, moaning so loud the tiny room turns into an echo chamber.

"Look at me, dear."

I manage to meet Stephanie's gaze, our eyes locked as I finish on her fingers. I catch my breath and whimper with each exhale, heart still pumping, adrenaline still making me see stars.

Eventually, sooner than I would have liked, she finishes and stands up. There's silence–that post sex glow fading like a setting sun. Steph looks at her hand, covered with familiar, white goop. If I had the energy I'd hide my face behind my hands— maybe even run right out of the changing room naked as the day I hatched.

Steph says nothing, looking at me with concern. "Do you need anything?"

My face is so hot— she's so hot with my mess dripping off her fingers onto the concrete. "You," I say smartly. "Again. Sometime."

Stephanie's mouth falls open, somehow surprised that I want to suffocate against her clit again. She leans in, her voice falling to a whisper. "Of course. You have my number for a reason."

She shakes out her hand, most of my mess blending into the concrete. We start pulling our swimsuits back on. She holds her hair up as I tie the strings of her bikini around her neck. Somehow this feels more intimate than sex.

We leave the changing room, not bothering to stagger our exit. Which backfires immediately, Carl is standing a yard away pushing a cart full of boxes. He looks at me and frowns with a furrowed brow. His brow slides further down his face as he looks at Stephanie, who hides her hands behind her back innocently. "I don't wanna know," he says finally and goes on his merry way.

Stephanie swallows. "You don't think he'll–"

"What? Tell people? Would that be such a bad thing?" I reach for her hand.

When she opens her mouth a bellowing roar rips through the country club. "Pool closed?!" I already know it's Lord Unnith. Stephanie and I distance ourselves and look in his direction. He stomps in my direction, smoke starting to drift from his nostrils. "Lydia?" My name sounds more like a warning.

I think fast. "Someone vomited."

Steph is even faster. "I vomited."

Unnith stands up straight. He doesn't really have lips but his mouth forms a hard line and the smoke has stopped. "I'm so sorry, Mrs. Donis. You do look flushed. Do you need me to call you a car?"

She shakes her head. "I'll be alright. I think I just need to get out of the sun." She looks back at me and breathes, "Thank you." With that she scurries off to gather her things she left poolside.

My eyes follow her like a lost puppy but Lord Unnith demands my attention. "Get this pool open. Looks like you've cleaned up most of it. Double-check the levels and get back up in that chair."

"Yes, sir," I say out of habit.

"*What?*"

"Yes… Lord Unnith."

Five minutes ago I was giving head and now all I have is a headache.

CHAPTER
Four

When are you free this week?

Whenever. The last shift ends at six so I can do whenever.

Alright. I want to see you again.

But I'll need a babysitter or to wait till it's Roman's weekend with the kids again.

Booo Roman!!!!

I don't know what you see in that guy.

It's a long story. I'm not sure I can quite remember what I saw in him either. But he cares about the kids. He's a good dad

We can talk about it over dinner.

Dinner? I'm blushing.

Are you? I've never seen you blush. I don't think I have.

> Does a Saturday reservation at Bistro 11 work?

> Absolutely.

———

AS SOON AS I hit send my stomach churns like a charybdis has just made my gut its summer home. Leaping from the couch I step into Jessie's room, the one with the biggest closet. Sitting on her bed she looks up from her phone but keeps quiet.

Sliding the door open I riffle through my clothes. Our arrangement is strange but makes sense when you remember the bathroom is my bedroom. All the storage in there is reserved for towels and toiletries, so I keep most of my clothes in Jessie's room. Not that I brought much besides shorts and t-shirts. Basic summer stuff.

Nothing nice enough for a dinner date at Bistro 11. I've never been, but everyone at school loves to talk about fine dining as if they've experienced it for themselves. Whoever writes food reviews sure deserves a raise because I know exactly what to order at Bistro 11. Fancy fish here I come. Assuming they let me in the door wearing the one body con dress I own. I'm pretty sure there is still a stain from the time I took an overconfident shot of amaro at a party.

Jessie drones. "I didn't touch your stuff." She doesn't look away from her phone. "Whatever it is you're looking for."

I huff. "I have nothing to wear."

She shrugs. "Less is more."

My lips scrunch as I consider if Jessie and I have a similar enough body type I can borrow something of her's. Except she has hips and breasts, very Human features, while I don't. I'm rail straight and flat as a board like every other Fishfolk. Maybe Goldie has something, but she's so thick with feathers…

I head to the balcony where Goldie sits in her nest facing the sun, her eyes closed and peaceful. I lean against the sliding door. "What's your dress size?"

She doesn't even open her eyes. "I dunno."

I stand there a while longer but Goldie doesn't offer any more information.

Inside, my phone buzzes with Steph's name scrawled across the screen. I answer. A childish voice shouts, "Hello!"

"Sophie? Is your mom there?"

Sophie giggles followed by a fumbling sound. Steph is in the background, asking Sophie to hand her the phone in a gentle voice. I purse my lips, holding back a laugh. There's more shuffling but finally Steph's voice comes through. "I'm so sorry about that—"

"Don't be, I actually need to talk to you."

"Oh? Do we need to reschedule?"

"Hopefully not." I chew the inside of my lip. "I just realized I don't have anything to wear. Like, I only packed shorts and t-shirts. Oh and swimsuits."

Steph hums. "A swimsuit might be nice." I swear I hear her wink through the phone. "How do you feel about a shopping trip, my treat?"

I blink. Did I just become a sugar baby? I hope so.

"I'm the one who picked such an upscale place, it's the least I can do. I don't imagine being a lifeguard pays much."

"I'm not exactly rolling in savings," I admit.

All my summer money is gone once the semester starts and I need a new set of textbooks. Never mind paying for housing or the lose-lose of chasing the college's dining option versus buying your own food. I have a classmate who crosses the river to do all his shopping because Jersey has a lower tax rate. Which leads to the whole class running a budget if he's actually saving any money once you account for travel costs.

"The kid's summer camp is finally starting up so I'm free during the day, when is your next day off?"

We coordinate a time while I poke around the bus schedule. Jessie is the only one with a car and I don't want to leave her and Goldie stranded. Plus that would entail me explaining who I'm meeting and why. Lying is a shit option. I'm still shocked our vomit fib hasn't come back to bite me in the ass— and Lord Unnith has some sharp teeth.

"So the bus leaves at eight so I should get there—"

"I'm picking you up," Steph says. "You think I wouldn't?"

I curl a strand of hair around my finger. "I just know you're busy."

"I am," she agrees. "But not so busy I can't drive you. I play chauffeur enough for my kids. At least with you we can listen to something other than Baby Shark."

"How do you know I don't love Baby Shark? He's my cousin actually."

She giggles, "Don't let Sophie know that. She's very into mermaids and the water right now." A muffled, sharp sound comes through. After the tenth time, I realize someone is saying "Ma" over and over again.

"I'll let you go, sounds like you've got kids to wrangle."

"Always," she sighs, but the devotion is still there. "See you soon."

She hangs up and I bring the phone to my chest. The word date has never popped up. Not in talking about the restaurant or going shopping together, but that's what's happening, isn't it? We're past hooking up. Steph is old enough I'm not sure situationship is really her speed. Then again after getting divorced from a grade A asshole, low commitment might be what she needs.

Goldie has a smile on her face. "Who was that?"

I slip my phone in my hoodie pocket. "Old friend."

"That didn't sound like catching up with an *old* friend."

Jessie pops her head out of her room. "Who?"

I'm not sure who to mean mug more, Jessie for being nosey or Goldie for eavesdropping. Instead, I grab my apartment keys. "Going for a walk. Text me if I should grab anything."

Outside I walk past storefronts alone with my thoughts. If you're really alone when one person occupies your mind. The thing is I'm not ready for a girlfriend. I'm not even ready to tell my roommates, who I'll probably never see again after this summer, that I've got a summer fling. My heart thuds as it hits me that the summer has just started and I'm already a mess for Steph.

Except I know we wouldn't work. Introducing me to her kids? Sure they know me, the same way kids know the old man next door and their pediatrician.

I'm just an adult. Not their step-mom. Roman certainly would have words. A Bunch of bullshit posturing phrases no one needs to hear.

There's still time to call things off— because ignoring my feelings worked so well last time….

Next time we hook up it won't be at my job. Already it's inevitable that we'll collide again. And again. And again. Till something gives out.

———

MOST MALLS ARE stark white voids with zero personality. This one, however, has beige marble floors that make a satisfying sound as dozens of women in heels walk across it. There's an orb shaped fountain that looks like something out of MOMA. All the shops are the sort of brand names you hear about on red carpets, Prada, Versache, Coach. They stand in stark contrast to the mall staples of H&M and the Gap to the point I wonder if they're just there to make the other stores look even more bougie.

It's more sterile than generic. "Kinda disappointed you didn't take me to the mall with the indoor water park," I tease Steph as I push my sunglasses up past my forehead.

Steph tsks, still wearing a large pair of tortoise shell sunglasses. "It's such a crap mall. Great if you want to tire out your kids but I'd rather just take them to Six Flags."

"Or you know, the park." My middle class might be showing but it needs to be said. Steph smiles, finally taking off her sunglasses.

We walk through the mall, taking in all the shops first before going inside any of them. I'm surprised by how many brands I've never heard of. My ex was always flipping through Vogue and talking about the next fashion trend. I thought I did a good job of listening, but now I'm not so sure.

I stop when I see a store with feminine mannequins styled both with dresses and suit-coats. Past them, inside the store proper, I can tell their clothing leads into neutral tones, nothing too flashy. Something I could probably wear again after my not-official-date with Steph. Next thing I know Steph's hand is around my wrist and she gently drags me into the store.

We're jumped by an employee. "Welcome in! Have you shopped with us before?"

"We haven't, we're looking for a dress." Steph turns to me.

"Um, yeah something fancy but not over the top." I wrack my brain for buzz words my ex would use. There's an array of floral designs on the dresses. "Garden party?"

The attendant nods and leads us to some couches near the dressing rooms. Steph leans over, grinning in my ear. "Garden party?"

"I don't really buy dresses," I admit. "Fashion is a mystery to me."

"We'll have to fix that." She leans back. "Appearances matter, especially in the workplace. You don't *need* a dress of course," she eyes a rack of women's jumpsuits. "But there is nothing worse than a poorly tailored suit."

"Suits are more my speed, not just the bathing kind."

Steph giggles just as the attendant comes back with a handful of dresses.

"Oh, can you do a little fashion show?" Steph holds her hands together like she's praying, her pretty pink fingertips at her lips.

Like I could ever muster the strength to say no to her.

The attendant helps me with the zippers and doesn't judge me too hard when I reveal I'm wearing a sports bra under my shirt. Every petite string looks awkward overtop black boxy straps. Still, each time I step out of the dressing room Steph lights up. I do little turns for her. Sway my hips to get a feel for the dress's flow. The fabrics are all so light it's like I'm wearing nothing at all.

When I step out wearing the last dress, Steph has a suit in her hands. She offers it to the attendant who slips past me back into the changing room. Steph walks up to me, taking my hands.

"This one is nice," she compliments. It's a light beige that matches her skin tone. Even where my scales are thinnest my skin has a blue undertone like the ocean is always beneath my skin.

"It would look nicer on you," I tell her.

"I have so many dresses I never wear…"

We've been here for a while but when I see the suit hanging in the changing room, it's like we've just gotten started. I keep a few shirt buttons open to expose my collar decorated with my scales. The black pants stop just above my ankle. I usually don't go for heels but I imagine a nice strappy pair would look nice. I leave the suit coat for last, the sleeves also a bit shorter than a man's suit.

For the first time I check myself out before letting Steph see me. Everything fits perfectly— but I admit I don't know what a well tailored suit looks like. Especially on my body.

When I step out, Steph gives me her glowing smile and breathes, "Wow."

I lift my chin with pride, leaving back on my heels.

"I wouldn't want to choose for you but—"

"This one," I agree.

When I change back into my shirts and shorts it's like Cinderella at midnight. One shopping trip and I can already feel how cheap and plastic my shirt is. It's an old freebie from some freshman event I attended forever ago. The logo has started to peel but the deep purple color pairs well with my scales. At least I think so.

My suit is folded and wrapped in tissue paper by the time we get up to the register. Steph pulls out a credit card and I lean over to get a look at it, trying to catch the company and memorize the plastic's color so I can look it up later.

Obviously Steph has money but it's rude to ask exactly how much money. Isn't it? My mom scolded me for asking all the kids on the playground how much money their parents made. She told that story over and over after I declared my business major. Kids being rude is funny, adults not so much.

"You hungry?" I ask Steph as we step outside the store. "Or do you need to do some more shopping."

"Need isn't the word I'd pick," she giggles. "But food is never a wasted expense."

"We can just do the food court," I tell her. "Something simple."

The two of us are shoulder to shoulder as we walk. "I haven't done the food court in ages," she admits.

Her knuckle brushes the back of my hand and I consider reaching for her. I wonder what we must look like to the people we pass. Certainly not mother and daughter, not that I'd be offended. Steph's genes are killer. Maybe step-mom and step-daughter?

It doesn't help that I still don't know what we are. Summer fling doesn't sit right with me. It's not even July yet but I know the summer will go by fast. Then what will we be?

A familiar Chinese restaurant is featured in the food court.

I pull Steph in that direction and she, once again, pulls out her credit card. I open my mouth to object but no sound comes out. I don't even reach for my wallet. Hardly a valiant effort but hey, I'm a college student. This is just wealth redistribution.

Maybe that's what we are, Marx's wet dream. Not that I've read any of his theories but I don't vibe with anything manifesto. It all feels a bit too self-congratulatory.

"Thanks for paying," I tell her as we sit down.

"Oh, of course," she says. A forkful of unnatural orange chicken is halfway to my mouth when she adds, "I like paying for you."

I tilt my head. "Careful, I might get used to getting spoiled."

Steph rests her chin in her palm. "Would that be such a bad thing?"

For a moment, all of the people and the rest of the food court disappears. The tiny table with Styrofoam boxes feels intimate, dare I say romantic. I keep telling myself we're not serious— keep trying to catch myself before I'm in too deep.

"I have something to tell you," Steph admits. "But not now." She sits up, shrugs her shoulders. "I want to save it for a real dinner."

"What, this isn't real?" I wave the fork of chicken like a magic wand.

Steph gives me a good-natured-grimace. "I'm not sure it is." She plucks the fork from between my fingers. "But who cares so long as it tastes good." She hums with content as she chews the basketball colored chicken.

We eat in silence for a while, but it feels like such a waste to finally have time with her and not say anything. "Do you work during the summer?"

"Less now versus the school year," she admits. "I work from home during the summer. I take a pay cut but it's worth it to spend more time with my kids."

"More time with you, less time with Roman."

She sighs, "It's not even that." She pokes at her noodles. "It's just so easy to lose track of time when you're working. At least, that's how it is for me. I get fixated— and it's never just one thing. You answer one email and by the time you're done you have five more. I like managing people but gosh, some of them are more needy than my kids." She smiles and shakes her head but it's a hollow expression.

"You're kids are pretty young and you're…" I hesitate, not wanting to be rude. "An older mom."

"I swear I look at Sophie's classmate's parents and half of them are teenagers. Except I know they aren't. Her daycare is much too expensive for that."

Again, I'm scared I'll come off as rude, like my little kid self at the playground. "I don't know how old you are," I admit. "I know you're older—"

"Because of the gray."

"Because older women are hotter," I shoot back.

Steph bites the edge of her lip. "Have you always preferred older women?"

"My first crush was the school librarian," I tell her. "I was maybe eight? No idea how old she was but she wore a chain on her glasses. Could have been in her twenties for all I remember."

"Could have been your age now…" Steph remarks. "How about we both say exactly how old we are?"

"Like, in months? I'll have to do a bit of math."

"No," she laughs. "I just don't know how old you are either. College age could mean anything."

"On three?" She nods. "One, two, three…"

"Forty-three."

"Twenty-one."

"You're younger than I thought," I blurt out. "I mean— you're just so well established—"

"Mhm," Steph nods. "Keep digging, dear. That answers another question I've had."

It's my turn to stare in silence. Steph gives me the courtesy of asking the question.

"Have you ever been with an older woman before?"

I shake my head. "I've only been with girls my age."

"You prefer to be called a girl, rather than a woman?" There's a familiar twinkle in her eye. It reminds me of wet bathing suits and kneeling before her.

"Yes, mommy?"

Steph fans herself, her cheeks already pink. Her voice is bubbly, almost a laugh."I'm blushing now, or getting a hot flash. Hard to tell at this age."

"You're not that old. You're just blushing because I'm so charming."

She lifts a brow, a smile persisting. "Well isn't that convenient for your ego?" We both laugh, she falters. Her eyes fall to the table. "I think I just wasted my youth. My twenties I was trying to get my foot in the door and my thirties were all spent trying to get ahead. Everything else was an after-thought."

I purse my lips, not sure how to lift her spirits. "Steven is… how old?" He's not a toddler and not a tween, somewhere between those vague ages.

"He's six. Sophie is four."

"So you didn't completely waste your time," I tell her.

"Oh God," she blocks her eyes with her hands. "Sorry," she chuckles. "I have to laugh, you've got me thinking about my love life a decade ago."

"Roman," I make sure his name is dripping with spite. Even stab a piece of chicken to really drive the point home.

Steph laughs. "Oh darling, it's even worse than that. Have you ever tried speed dating? Does that even exist?"

"Maybe?" I offer. "I've heard of it. Wait, is that how you two met?"

She nods. "It's funny what a terrible impression people can make in such a short amount of time. I'll never forget this one man, he handed me his business card! On a date! A five minute date but the last thing I wanted to think about was *work*. I tore it up right then and there but we still had four minutes on the clock. It was terrible."

I think of stuff a straight man would do. "At least no one tried to do close up magic."

Steph is silent.

"Did someone actually?"

"He handed out so many feather flowers. I can admit, I was a bit impressed. Less by the magic and more the commitment."

"But you ended up with," I pause to get the right amount of rasp in my throat, "*Roman*."

"He was nicer back then. I chose to remember him as being nicer."

"What did you see in him?" I ask. "Or was it less about his insides and more about his outsides?"

"Neither. He said he wanted kids. *Really* wanted kids. I wanted kids. We had kids. We got divorced." It's all very matter of fact. "Maybe I should have seen that coming…"

"That's a big thing to agree on," I assure her, like I've got any authority. Marriage doesn't interest me, never has. "And your kids are cool, so I guess Roman isn't the *absolute* worst."

Maybe I should admit that kids don't really interest me either. Treat this like a speed date and get all our plans out of the way.

It's like she's reading my mind. "You like kids?"

I opt for honesty. "Not really. I don't hate them, I don't love them either."

She nods. "It's good you know that. I swear some of the other moms don't like kids. Of course I'd never say that to another mom."

"Hey, if you ever want to gossip, I'm all ears. I love drama I'm not a part of."

We finish up eating and head back to Steph's car. As we enter the car park, she checks her watch. "I have to pick up the kids in half an hour."

"Do you have enough time? I can take the bus home."

"Could you? Gosh, I'm sorry I lost track of time, I just really wanted to have lunch with you."

A warm breeze pushes some hair into her face. She reaches to push it behind her ear, but I'm faster. My fingers brush the back of her ear. "Don't worry about it." I let my hand linger near her face.

"Remind me that we'll see each other soon."

I chuckle. "Well yeah, we'll see each other at the pool. You'll get to spoil me at dinner in my nice suit."

She tilts her head, cheek now resting in the palm of my hand. "I just wanted to hear you say that."

CHAPTER
Five

IT'S my first time on lake duty, so of course that would be the day a dozen middle school aged kids all decide to take some tubes out. It's not really tubing if there isn't an actual current, is it? Anyway, a bunch of kids with braces and awkward haircuts scream their heads off. They shout a bunch of nonsense that makes the other kids cackle. It must be some internet thing I'm too old to understand.

Lake policy is that anyone going past their shoulders must wear a lifejacket. Some of the kids make me nervous, bobbing in the water like a buoy. Running out of stamina is easy, especially in the summer heat. Thankfully every kid manages to get themselves back to the shore without assistance.

When I leave to take my break I scan the pool to look for Stephanie. It's pretty packed today, and I spot plenty of sun hats and black bathing suits but none of the women have bright pink nails or eye-catching gray hair. Once I'm clocked out I linger in the supplies hallway, grabbing my phone to text her and ask if she's stopping by today.

"Hey," Carl drones.

My phone fumbles out of my hands but I manage to catch it before it hits the ground.

Carl leans against the metal shelving. "Who you texting?"

"Your mom."

Damn it– those middle schoolers got to me.

"Funny you mention *moms*…"

It hits me then, the memory of Carl catching me and Steph as we left the changing room. He said he didn't want to know. Except no one says that unless they think something nefarious is happening.

I cross my arms. "Look I only have a thirty-minute break so if you could make this lecture quick?"

"Wow. Snippy much?" He pushes off the shelves. His hands rest on his hips. "Just don't be obvious, okay? The last thing I need is a bunch of cougars thinking it's open season on the pool boys."

I roll my eyes. "Oh please. My ass is already halfway out in this suit."

Carl tilts his head "If you want modesty shorts go right ahead. Lord Unnith won't notice and I don't care so long as it won't obstruct you during a rescue."

I keep my arms crossed despite getting what I've wanted since I started working here.

"You know I really should write you up for having sex on the property."

"Whose having sex on the property?" Jessie struts in, pushing past me to clock out. "It's not Daddy Unnith again is it?"

"Excuse me?" I choke. From the lack of reaction on Carl's part, I'm guessing *Daddy* is another regal title Unnith doesn't mind. Or that's just the staff nickname for him.

Carl rubs his temples. "I have given up on trying to wrangle that man."

"Not to sound like a poolside mom on her fourth glass of wine but *what?*" I turn to Jessie, knowing. "You've gotta explain."

Jessie's expression is so bland compared to her words.

"Two summers ago, people kept having affairs in the bushes. We used to do cocktail nights– super fancy, I guess all that champaign made people a little frisky."

"Lord Unnith took a little roll in the hay? Er, the bushes?"

"Let's change the subject," Carl suggests.

Jessie keeps talking. "Yeah but we never found out who he was with. Apparently Juan, he doesn't work here anymore, but Juan saw his tail sticking out to the bushes. Someone else with a membership must have spotted him too because we stopped doing cocktail nights after that summer."

I rock back on my heels. "So… who else got caught with shrubbery up their ass?"

Jessie shrugs. "My guess is any members who got divorced in the last two years still have some leaves suck up their crack."

Steph pops into my mind, not that she's ever really gone. She's never told me why her and Roman split. The guy is an aggressive jerk, but plenty of guys like that are in loveless marriages. I don't like picturing his face but I can see him being the type to get some shitty handjob in the bushes while his breadwinner wife is inside. What an ass.

I'm quite literally pulled from my thoughts as Jessie takes my wrist and leads me out of the supply hallway. Carl glares at me as we go. Something about all that spite coming from a single eye makes it super intense.

Jessie giggles as we grab out lunches from the staff fridge.

"You've worked here a long time, right?" I ask.

"Since I was sixteen."

"You must be pretty close with some of the families here."

"Um…" Jessie hesitates. "Well my parents were members here too so… yeah I know the regulars. Not so much anymore. People move. People stop coming."

We head outside to the staff-reserved picnic table. "People catch their husbands getting sucked off in the bushes and get divorced?"

"Exactly," Jessie nods.

I poke at my lunch and think about how soon I'll be having a much nicer meal with Steph. Then wonder if Roman of all fucking people broke her heart for a quickie. Unless... Steph wouldn't have an affair. Would she?

I need to change the subject. "I didn't realize you grew up around here."

"Sort of. My step-father had a place in town. Ex-step father, if you catch my drift."

"Pretty hard to misunderstand that statement." This conversation is making me lose my appetite. Back home people don't get divorced. Which isn't a good thing. I guess when your options are sharing a life with someone you dislike or a bunch of lawyers and paperwork, I'll take the lawyers. "But you still work here?"

"Daddy Unnith takes care of me," she winks, then cackles. "Sorry, that's just what people call him."

"I don't think Carl calls him that."

"Because Carl is a stick in the mud. He's great at his job, honestly, he's not even that strict with us, he just never has any fun."

I continue to pick at my food, not sure if I should tell Jessie what he told me. She has no idea about me and Steph. Well, I haven't told her anything. Maybe Carl is right and I'm being too obvious. Jessie has teased me about staring at the moms sitting poolside. "I can't hate a guy for being serious about his job."

"He's just *so* serious. You gotta be able to turn that on and off," Jessie argues.

"Maybe you're not serious enough," I shrug.

"About a summer job?"

"That you've had for five years."

Jessie blinks like she's never considered that fact before. Funny how we can know things without ever actually thinking about their repercussions.

I try to walk back my statement. "If you've had the position for this long, you're doing something right."

"Or Unnith just feels bad for me."

"Come on, he wouldn't let you be a *lifeguard* out of pity."

Jessie frowns. "Rich folks love a charity case." I try to tell her that's not at all what she is but she keeps talking. "They love talking about charity even more. Trust me, Lydia, everyone here is playing chess while we're playing checkers. When someone is more pressed about income tax than paying for groceries or car payments, their brain just works different." She reaches into my salad and stabs a clementine. "But it's not all bad. I'm still close with my step-brother. He's like, not someone I'd be friends with if we hadn't been related for a few years, but I feel like he gets me the way siblings do."

I start eating so I don't have to talk. Offering myself time to really think about what Jessie has said. NYU isn't cheap. I've seen the rich kids who pay for dining but do takeout for every meal regardless. The girls who have a different designer handbag every semester. Kids who talk about private jets like its economy class. I never even took a plane till I moved out here.

Give me enough time with a jet, Rolls-Royce, and mommy's money and I'd start thinking differently too.

———

I'VE ADJUSTED my shirt collar ten times in the last minute. Steph texted ten minutes ago that she's on her way. Since then I've been hiding out in Jessie's room getting ready.

The suit is still as crisp as it was the day at the mall. I've got my blonde hair up in a messy bun– but not too messy. The sort of messy you see on magazine covers. I've bothered with some jewelry, a gold medallion with a replica Atlantean coin I bought ages ago and the faux pearl earrings I bought for interviews. I don't own heels so black ballet flats will have to do. They make me feel so childish but stumbling down the street in a fresh pair of stilettos wouldn't be much better.

My chest is so tight. I haven't felt this anxious since my internship interviews. Except this isn't a job interview– there aren't any other candidates for Steph's attention. *She likes you enough to buy you a suit,* I remind myself.

There's a faint buzzing and I snatch my phone from the bedside table. Steph is outside. I chew the inside of her lip. Before I leave I crack the door just wide enough to peer into the living room. Jessie and Goldie are sitting on the couch, Jessie's fingers are deep in Goldie's feathers as they chat.

I step out and march to the front door, not in the mood to strike up a conversation with them.

"Woah!" Goldie chirps.

Still preening Goldie's feathers Jessie turns her head. "You look nice."

"You look hot." Goldie grins.

Jessie snaps back to Goldie, her eyes wide.

"Just grabbing some drinks with a friend." It's not a complete lie. Steph is a friend. Not quite a girlfriend. Just a friend with benefits, but that's a mouthful. I don't linger, afraid of any follow up questions.

Lucky for me Jessie is too interested in picking Goldie's brain along with her feathers. "You think she looks hot?"

The sky is a pale orange, the sun just starting to set. I scan for Steph's car, looking for the silver SUV she picked me up in a few days ago. Instead a black car, small and low to the ground, lowers its window. "Hello dear," a voice calls.

I bend over, looking inside to see a familiar pair of sunglasses flanked by streaks of grey. She smiles and I smile back. I slide into the passenger's seat. There are no other seats. "Practical," I tease.

Steph pulls away from the curb, the engine making a satisfying purring noise. "I tell everyone I'm going to trade it in but to be honest, I like having something for myself."

The other trucks and vans are so much taller than us. As cool as this car is, it's meant for solitary drives along the beach or in the woods. Not the turnpike.

"You know the second Steven turns sixteen he'll want to take this for a spin." I tell her.

"Hm, maybe by then he can have it. In eleven years cars will be, what, self driving? Hovering? Make you martinis?"

"I guess every kid needs a clunker car to start."

Steph laughs as she switches to the far left lane. The engine's purr amps up to a proper roar as we speed down the highway toward the city.

"Bridge or tunnel?" I ask as if I haven't relied on the train every time I leave the city.

"Holland tunnel," she specifies. "I avoid midtown at all costs."

Somehow she manages to drift across three lanes to get us to the offramp for the tunnel. Steph is a smooth driver but I find myself clawing her nice leather seats. I'm so glad I didn't bother with a car when I moved out here. Being a passenger princess is stressful as is, never mind actually driving.

The traffic in Manhattan is steady, constantly moving and consistently crowded. The subway and sidewalks are the same. I find those to be less stressful than the road. As we cruise down 41st Street Steph touches my arm. "Nervous?"

Great. She probably thinks I'm scared about our date. "You're a really good driver. I could never drive down Manhattan."

She puts her hand back on the steering wheel. "I forget all of this is unusual to most people."

"Most people would be more focused on the beautiful woman with the fancy car driving them. I'm just bad at prioritizing." I try to focus on the buildings. It's hard to tell what's for business and what's for pleasure. Every wall is covered in glass, some tinted dark while others you can see into. "Any of these building's yours?"

"Oh, the restaurant is right across from where I work. I'm sort of a regular there."

"Do regulars at Bistro 11 get special treatment? An extra dinner mint?"

Steph purses her lips and smiles. "There should be a crème brûlée set aside just for me. They're rather popular."

"And it would be such a shame if their regular didn't get her favorite dessert," I finish.

Steph tilts her head back with pride. "I never made any demands, mind you. Though the kitchen can see out into the dining room. So the kitchen staff might have noticed my pout in the past."

Steph makes a sharp turn into an underground parking garage. "Parking. The great equalizer." As we roll down the ramp we get in line along with a minivan and another nice looking car. A dad wearing a yankees jersey is arguing with one of the attendants, his family standing nearby. I like to think I've gotten pretty good at recognizing tourists. Not that they're ever subtle about it.

Soon a parking attendant meets us and Steph hands him her keys. I walk to her side and she's quick to slip her arm into mine. We start walking, but I look back to watch the stranger drive off with Steph's car. "How do you trust they won't scratch it?"

Steph laughs, "how can I trust that I wont? These guys park hundreds of cars a day for people with bigger tempers than me. Besides, it's their job. No one intentionally messes up their job."

As we walk Steph notices my shoes. "Comfortable?"

"They're the only thing I own that aren't sneakers." I admit.

She hums to herself. "Should have bought you some loafers at the mall. Maybe a good pair of oxfords…"

All this talk of fashion has me looking her up and down. I hadn't gotten a good look at her outfit till now. She's wearing an emerald dress made of velvet. In some lighting it looks black. The dress is long, tight against the curves of her hips, with a slit down the side that allows her to strut her thick legs. The top part of the dress is sculpted with short sleeves, a Queen Anne cut, I think it's called. Steph always looks amazing but she's all dressed up tonight. Dressed for me…

Inside the restaurant Steph gives her name to the host, but judging by his smile I think he already knows who she is. As we're led to the table I struggle to take it all in. Everything is so crisp, clean, and bright– not the low lighting I expected. The bar wall is shelves upon shelves of bottles, with names I've never heard of. Brands of liquor they don't sell at bodegas or the grocery store. The waiters are all dressed in vests and dark pants. We pass a loud table with men in suits clearly having just left the office.

Next thing I know we're at our table, the host pulling out Steph's chair before reaching for mine. I sit before he grabs the back of the chair. I'm not sure what compels me to do this. It's already obvious that I don't belong here. Everyone looks at least a decade older than me and are so comfortable, they only have to glance at the menu.

Steph and I don't even have a moment to talk before a waiter arrives and asks if we would like a drink.

"Do you like wine?" Steph tilts her head affectionately.

"Yes," I say, but the only wine I can think of is strawberry pink and from a box. If their wall of bottles is any indicator of their stock, I doubt they have any boxes in the back.

"We'll have a bottle of the Coriole." The waiter leaves. "You can order whatever drink you like, I just love Australian wines."

I nod, feeling stiffness in my neck. The wine appears as if pulled out of a magician's hat and it takes all my self control not to down my glass to settle my nerves. Still, I take such a huge gulp of the stuff I might as well be drinking it straight from the bag.

I've already scoped out the menu online but read it anyway. Everything is familiar but alien. There are dishes that sound simple enough, ravioli for example, till I read the description and fail to recognize half the ingredients. How am I supposed to know the difference between a Bianchetto and a Burgundy truffle? Does anyone actually know or do they just pretend to know?

"I think I'll ask what the chef recommends."

Steph nods, holding her glass of wine with grace. "Always a good option. They know what's freshest. Not to mention we haven't heard the specials yet." Behind her there is a clear view into the kitchen, which is even more pristine than the dining room. The chefs are all clad in white like fresh snow. A Dragonfolk with black scales patrols the kitchen, stopping to dip a small spoon into a skillet and taste whatever is being made.

I could watch the chefs dance around each other for hours but Steph's voice pulls me back. "Do you have any dietary restrictions?"

"I prefer fish, but I'm not picky. Not allergic to anything."

"It's silly, but I wasn't sure if Fishfolk could eat meat."

"Fish is meat," I tell her with a sly look. "And I'm from the midwest. Of course I can eat beef."

"I didn't know you were from the midwest," Steph smiles. "Let me guess, close to the great lakes?"

"Lake Huron. I grew up in Michigan. Small lakeside town no one has ever heard of. We're not even a vacation spot."

"You don't want to be. Seasonal tourists are the worst. My grandparents lived out on the shore, summers with them were always so chaotic with all the tourists."

"Jersey girl?"

Steph's grin is so infectious I smile as well. "Born and

raised. Proud of it too. Even if as soon as I had an allowance for it I hightailed to the city. But things were different then."

"You mean *more* dangerous?" I raise a brow. "I've read about what Times Square used to be."

"I told you, I hate midtown! Always have, always will. I just wanted to visit the museums."

"Uh-huh," I hum as I take another sip of my wine.

"I was a good girl."

I quirk a brow. "No one who says that is ever a good girl."

"Well," she rolls her shoulders back, "I suppose you know me a bit too well."

The waiter returns and Steph opens her mouth before shutting it like a trap. "We haven't discussed appetizers."

"I trust you. You're a regular here, isn't she?" I look at the waiter.

The waiter doesn't miss a beat. "We're very grateful to have Mrs. Donis dine with us regularly."

"Smooth," I deadpan. "You must get good tips."

"I try, Miss."

Steph says, "We'll have to have the crudo, whatever fish the chef recommends. And I know it sounds basic but the hummus platter is actually amazing."

We're alone again. Hopefully for some time. "You mentioned something at the mall that you wanted to talk about?"

Steph's cheeks go pink. "Yes," her voice is serious. I feel like I'm in a board meeting as she explains. "I want to propose a relationship between us. Not girlfriends…"

I frown. "Okay…"

"I've only been divorced for a year now. To be honest, things between me and my ex– well, you've seen how we are. I made a mistake marrying him. One that's hard to really regret because Steven and Sophie are my world. Them and my job but I'm trying to make work a bit less of a priority right now."

I nod, not sure if I should speak.

"I like being single. But I also like you."

"You like fucking me." I say.

Steph keeps up, not at all phased by my bluntness. "*We* like fucking each other. Or am I wrong?"

I purse my lips. Steph takes a slow, steady breath.

"If we were the same age, Lydia, I would have been so intimidated by you. You know who you are, what you want. I'm dying to see where you are in five years, how you'll soar wherever it is you land."

I try not to let the complement go to my head. "You want to mentor me?"

"Oh we're past that dear. What with the taste of you still on my tongue. I want to give you all the tools to cut through the bullshit. Take some ease off the stress that comes with being a young professional. I want to spoil you– not just with my body."

My tongue drags across my bottom lip. I too can still taste her sweetness.

"The arrangement isn't anything too creative." She picks up her wine, rolling her wrist so the liquid sloshes against the sides. "You see something you like, you send it to mommy. You get to walk around in, I don't know, diamond tennis bracelets or Hermés whatever. And I get you all to myself." Steph takes a big gulp of wine and I realize just how much courage it must have taken to lay it all out on the table like that.

"So we'd be exclusive?"

She runs a finger along the bottom base of her wine glass. "I won't see anyone else. I don't have the time or the energy to date. If someone came into your life you wanted to see, and they were comfortable with our arrangement..." Her eyes roll around in her head, not sarcastically, she's clearly thinking of logistics. "But then there's STIs and what not to worry about."

"You said you want me all to yourself."

"When we're together, like this, I expect to have you all to myself. I expect when we set a date that you arrive, that you won't think about classes or work or other women… I know I can't fulfill your emotional needs, Lydia." She looks at the table, at her left hand where a ring should be. "So I offer you what I have. A body and a bank account."

"You're more than that," I breathe.

"I know," she lets out a humorless laugh. "I'm also a mother, a divorcee, a woman getting closer to fifty every day. Are you ready for those things, Lydia? Seriously ready for that to be your life?"

I stop and actually think about what she's saying. Steph is too nice to say it to my face but I'm not ready for the responsibilities that come with her current life.

I don't want kids. I don't want to waste my weekends at soccer games and make small talk with other parents. I don't want to wave to neighbors that gossip about me behind my back. I don't want to go to dinner parties and have to lie through my teeth when people ask how we met. All I want is Steph. But Stephanie exists. Stephanie has responsibilities and girlfriends share that burden. How many all-nighters did I pull with my ex because *she* forgot she had an essay due the next day?

"I will be someday…"

"Someday…" Steph replies wistfully.

I don't even want to get married. I don't tell her that. To be honest there are pretty few people who know that about me— my ex, a few close friends… I've seen too many couples back home who shouldn't be together and too many bitter exes out East. Let me just love someone in peace. Why should anyone, especially the government, get involved? Nothing says sensual like paperwork.

The waiter arrives with our appetizers and I'm surprised that Steph dives right in, scooping up hummus with a slice of pita. I snag a piece of crudo and pop it in my mouth, the fish so thin it melts in my mouth. "Wow…" I say rudely, the fish still on my tongue.

Steph just giggles and gets another scoop of hummus.

I can't let the issue lie for long. "You know I'm not all that interested in bracelets and suits."

"I know you aren't, but your future boss might. When you intern they'll expect you to look the part."

Cutting through all the bullshit.

"What if I want a little treat? Like a ten dollar coffee?"

"Dear, I'll let you buy coffee for you and your friends and your friend's friends." She finally dives into the crudo.

I've wondered about something for a while but never had the chance to ask. "How much are you worth?" It's such a rude question, but Steph doesn't balk at it.

"All my assets, real estate, cars, stocks, a few fine art pieces, are worth ten million."

It's a good thing I didn't go for a bite of food waiting for her to respond because I absolutely would have choked on it. The number alone is staggering but her utter indifference is even more baffling. *Ten million.* That's tuition for one hundred NYU Stern students with a good chunk left over. That's a beach house on every major body of water in the United States. There's fuck you money and then there's fuck your whole bloodline money.

And here she is munching away on fish with me sitting slack jawed across from her.

It almost feels too late to ask, but I go for it anyway. "Why?"

Steph chews her fish for a moment before responding. "You know how they say, what do you buy for the woman who has everything? That's how I feel with myself. Believe me, when you say you're not interested in fancy jewelry or name brand suits, I'm pretty over them as well. I could invest, more than I already have, but why let my accountant have all the fun?"

"You don't get your rocks off watching numbers go up and down?"

She sighs, "If only… Nowadays the only thing that gets me going is pretty blond girls with scales like moonstones."

I roll my eyes to try and ignore that my stomach is doing somersaults. "Why not spoil your kids?"

Her brows furrow. "Because I don't want to raise little brats. My kids will know the word *no*. But… it might be fun if you're a little bratty."

Funny she mentions the word no when I find it impossible to deny her. "I don't see that happening. I like you too much."

"And I like you. I'm so torn between wishing I met you sooner and feeling like here and now is perfect. That this is our moment."

Our appetizer plates are empty, only a scarce amount of hummus clinging to the serving dish. The waiter reappears.

"I might be getting ahead of myself," Steph admits. "I'll have the truffle ravioli," she says to the waiter so casually it gives me whiplash.

He looks at me expectantly. "The halibut." I say just to get him to go away. "Just so I understand the arrangement; you buy me what I want, we go on dates with happy endings, but without the emotional baggage of a standard relationship."

Steph nods. "I'm also not sure if we should be public about it."

"We're in public now." I say just to be a wise ass and see her reaction. It's one thing to go out to a crowded mall or a New York City restaurant. It's another thing to hold hands poolside at the country club. "You're not interested in some arm candy?"

Steph purses her lips, thinking. "I am… but to start, let's keep things quiet. That is, if you want to go through with this." A pause. "I'm sorry if this is forward. If you feel like you can't say no."

"Even before tonight, before everything, I don't think I

could say no to you." Except I still haven't said *yes*. Where is this hesitation coming from? I'm good with casual sex and I don't want to play step-mom. Getting everything I want from her makes this all feel unfair. As if any relationship is completely equal, like every relationship isn't just a tad trans-actional.

I sigh and take a sip of wine. "Alright," I say finally, gesturing to Steph with my glass. "Anything I want, you can provide. But I'm still going to work."

Steph nods. "Oh, of course."

"And I think we should reassess when the summer ends. I'm pretty busy during the school year and it sounds like you'll be pretty swamped after the summer as well."

Steph's lips are a hard line. "This is true..."

A laugh bubbles up from the back of my throat. "A summer sugar baby. Beats an unpaid internship that's for sure."

She relaxes, even smiling a little. Then she raises her wine glass. "To the summer."

The lip of my glass meets hers with a soft *clink*. "To the summer."

Dinner is amazing, the aroma alone better than anything I've ever experienced. The halibut is so soft and buttery, not quite the same as the flavorful crudo but still delicious. Steph lets me have a truffle ravioli. I wasn't sure what to expect. The truffle's rich, earthy flavor is so different from anything I've ever eaten before.

"If we ever come back, I'm ordering pasta." I decide.

"Just say the word and we can be right back here," Steph reminds me.

I get what I want now. All I have to do is ask.

Which might be harder than I realized.

Steph pays and while I'm curious how much this all costs I don't look at the bill. Tonight has been nice and I don't need to stuff guilt down my already full stomach. Even if the cost is nothing to Steph, even with our arrangement, I still need time to wrap my head around it.

As we step onto the sidewalk I turn to walk to the parking garage. My arm tugs on Steph, who stands still. She points at the skyscraper across from the restaurant. "Would you like to see my office?"

I've been in office buildings, which sounds so drab, but the offices in the city are awe inspiring. Even if every time I've been in one I've been a shaking mess right before an interview, which puts a downer on the skyline views and manicured space.

So I nod, letting Steph guide me across the street to the office. To *her* office. She pulls a keycard from her purse. There's a receptionist, but based on his build I assume he's here to kick people out and not check people in. He gives Steph a nod and pays me no mind.

Last time I stepped into a building like this I had to give them a bunch of information, they even took my photo. Maybe since its past office hours security is lax? I don't get a chance to ask. The second Steph and I are in the elevator, her lips are on mine.

She tastes sweet like wine. Her hips push me against the wall of the elevator, not that I fight back. Instead I grab her ass, the velvet rough against my palms. While I claw at her, she touches my cheek, holding it like it's something precious. Steph pulls her lips from mine with a gasp, "I couldn't wait." Her chest heaves as she breathes. "Till upstairs–" I lean over to find her lips again.

The elevator dings before it stops, sooner than I would have liked. Steph takes my hand and leads me out. I grab her ass as she skips and she lets out a girlish giggle. Fluorescent lights blink on, catching our movements. We enter a room full of cubicles, but Steph walks right past them. She leads me to a glass wall, the office inside on full display. Next to the door is a plaque that reads "Stephanie Donis Senior Director of Marketing Analytics."

Inside the office, it's my turn to jump on her, pushing her toward the desk. My hands meet the desktop, pinning her in place as I kiss her neck. Working down to her collar, running my tongue down the space between her breasts. "Oh my God," Steph breathes. "You're distracting me." She grabs my hair bun and yanks, forcing me to look up at her.

Her cheeks are flush while her lips sparkle with saliva. "I have something I want to do…" Her other hand settles under my chin. "Remember how good mommy treats you…"

"How could I forget?" I tilt my head to kiss her fingertips. "Tell me."

"As handsome as you look in that suit– take it off."

I step back and pull at the buttons of my shirt. Steph leans against the desk, her half-lidded eyes trailing down my body. Her closed lip smirk makes me want to know what she has planned. But clothes first. I was in a rush to get everything off but I take the time to fold my shirt and pants, setting them down on her desk. As if I would let my gift from Steph be abandoned on the floor.

As I lay my suit coat over the desk, Steph strokes my arm with her knuckle. I'm naked, wearing nothing but fake pearls and a gold chain.

"Have I told you how much I love your scales?" Steph asks. "They remind me of the ocean."

I smile to myself and nod, for once just soaking up her complement.

"Stand by the window," Steph tells me. Though the entire wall looking out over the city is one big window. Steph's office, I realize, is just a glass container. Like a fish tank. It must be hard to work all day knowing you have zero privacy.

I stand at the window. The New York skyline is alive with yellow light from windows, colorful LEDs catching my atten-tion before losing it just as quick, so many famous landmarks laid out before me. Then I notice Steph in the window's reflection, stalking up behind me.

She takes my hip and gently pushes me forward so my body is pressed up against the glass. Her chest is so warm against my bare back. I take a shaky breath, the glass cold but nothing I can't handle. Her chest is hot against my bare back, her skin smooth like the inside of a seashell.

Steph runs a hand along my ass before dipping a finger inside me. "So wet already," she praises. One finger works me slowly, coaxing and curling inside me.

"What if someone sees?" I choke though we're fifty stories up. There are plenty of tall buildings around us– someone could look across the skyline and spot us.

But Steph just chuckles against my neck. "That's exactly what I want." Another finger slips inside me. "For everyone to see my darling." Her fingers press against my walls, just below my g-spot and I arch my back. "So impatient," Steph giggles before nipping at my neck.

"What happened to private?" I tease. Her little nibbles turn into a proper bite, right where my neck meets my collar. I gasp and it fades into a moan. I wonder, hope even, she leaves her mark.

She starts pumping her fingers and presses her chest to my back. Trapped against her and the window. I whimper, keeping my lips shut tight. Steph tsks. "Why are you being so shy? Mommy wants to hear you, sugar."

I gasp before all the air escapes me in a shriek of pleasure. Steph rewards me by reaching forward and pushing aside my tentacles to play with my clit. "Fuuuck," I drone. I rock my hips what little I can, my thighs slapping against the glass. Forget subtly— I want everyone, this whole city, to see how Steph fucks me.

Steph giggles, "What a cute little Guppy." My tentacles wrap around her wrist, desperate to keep her there. "Don't cum till mommy says."

I groan, but manage to say, "yes, mommy." It's the least I can do after everything she's given me: dinner, a nice suit, some of the best sex I've ever had. And I'll get to have it, over and over again, I just have to ask. Not beg– ask.

Steph stuffs me with another finger, fulling me up to her knuckle. She jerks her hand fast and I start to see stars. "Fuck-fuck!" Her fingers rub my clit just as fast.

"Don't finish just yet, dear." Her voice is calm in my ear. "I can't get enough of your moans." She presses her nose to my neck. "So pretty when you ride my fingers…"

I bite down on my lip– not to stifle my sounds but to ground me. Holding on for dear life not wanting to disappoint her. To misbehave and make mommy angry. But finally she rescues me, "Finish for me, dear. Make a mess on my fingers."

My knees shake and I brace myself against the window. My clit tightens, then relaxes and begins dripping. The cold glass feels good against my cheek as I finish on her digits, feeling my slick drip between my thighs. Despite the glass my cheeks grow hot, embarrassed as my slick and eggs slide down my leg about to make a mess of the carpet.

Steph finally pulls her hand back, chuckling to herself. "I love how much there is…" she says wistfully, looking at her fingers and palm covered with a white, milky substance. She steps away and grabs some tissues from her desk. She catches the mess on my calf before cleaning herself up.

My heart thuds in my ears, the New York skyline wavering. Steph strokes my hair, pulling me back away from the window and to a nearby couch. She settles me into her lap, then pulls aside the front of her dress. Her bra is the same emerald green of her dress and lacy. Cupping her heavy breast she hoists it out of her bra cup and brings it to my mouth.

I suck, running the flat of my tongue across her nipple. I

reach for her other breast and massage it, running circles around the lace. "There…" she purrs. "Just relax now…"

I lose track of time. Lose myself as I lick at her breast, admiring how her skin stretches to accommodate them. Forget about everything when she strokes my hair and looks at me with eyes so full of… what I'm not sure. Whatever it is, it makes me feel safe.

CHAPTER
Six

JULY IS IN FULL SWING. If the heat wasn't a dead giveaway, the dozens of bodies filling the pool would do the trick. The days go by faster now that there's more people to watch but the job actually becomes easier. A lot of siblings tell their younger siblings not to run. Everyone is cautious when jumping into the pool, not wanting to injure themselves or others. I watch a lot of drunk adults take naps instead of a dip in the pool.

Still, I don't have time to gawk at Steph. She mostly sticks to the kiddie pool and shallow end. I make it a point to scan the entire pool. It's foolish to think accidents only happen in the deep end, when the shallow waters allow for more scrapes and bruises. Never-mind little kids and their messes. I had to explain to a girl around my age holding a cherub toddler that there is a difference between diapers and swim diapers.

The glamor of it all.

I start to get to know the regulars, not just Steph. There's Carol, the old lady who likes to do laps early in the morning before the afternoon rush, and Hari a Snake Person who always brings his extended family to the pool. Their entire bottom halves are snake tails so they slither through the water and complain about the chlorine drying their scales almost as much as I do.

Then there's Roman. I refuse to call him a regular, but he's been showing up more now. Somehow he has a membership despite not living in town. Grandfathered in I guess. I try to ignore him, but I can feel his eyes on me while I sit on the elevated chair. I hope he gets a neck cramp.

I'm finishing up my break when we bump into each other inside. The air conditioning whirrs, blowing icy air onto the both of us. I scowl. "I hate to ask when I'm off duty, but who is watching your kids?"

Roman frowns. "My friend Tiffany. Steph didn't get *everything* in the divorce."

I hate that he calls her Steph. My disgust is obvious because he makes a face right back.

"Does she have you watching me or something?"

"No, I just don't like guys who yell at their ex wives. It's completely personal." I should have just left it there, pushed past him and gotten back to work. But his stupid face is getting red, staring at his cheeks and creeping up to his ears. So I push. "Looks like you could use a cocktail, Roman."

He frowns. "That supposed to mean something?"

"No, nevermind. Just rumors."

"Steph telling people I cheated?" He huffs.

"You really need to get off Steph's ass." I tell him. "There's plenty of gossips poolside."

"Don't believe everything you hear, girlie."

I cross my arms. "Girlie? Alright, well, this girlie has to get back to work." Finally I step past him and head back to the pool.

It's like my body moves but my mind stays behind, fixated now on Roman. I never said he cheated, he offered up that tidbit himself. It's not something I want to talk to Steph about. Our arrangement is fun. It's supposed to be *fun*, not dig into each other's lives and unearth all the trauma we worked so hard to hide.

When the sun hits my face I tell myself to drop it, sliding my glasses down over my eyes. Jessie sits on the chair with her chin in her hands, looking bored despite the controlled chaos around her. "Here to take over," I tell her.

"Finally!" She hops down, "I'm dying for some coffee. You want me to get you anything?"

"In this heat?" I pause my climb up to the chair. "Hell no."

As I settle in, Jessie starts acting like we're both clocked out. "You got any plans this weekend?"

I lift a brow even if she can't see it from her vantage. "Sleep. Watch my favorite problematic YouTube lesbians." I lie. I plan to text Steph, she doesn't have the kids this weekend but we haven't made any solid plans to meet up yet.

"Wrong, you're coming to a bonfire party."

I lower my sunglasses but before I can say *excuse me*, she continues.

"Goldie is coming too. It's a bunch of local kids all back from college. There will be so much—" She stops herself, remembering we are at work and that for what Carl lacks in sight he makes up for with hearing. "Free goodies."

"Fine," I deadpan, accepting this is part of our roommate contract. "I'll be there."

"You won't regret it!" With that she leaves with pep in her step.

I roll my eyes, which is unfair. Jessie is being nice. I'm the loser roommate whose friends are all too busy with internships or went back home for the summer. If she invited me out of pity, she did a good job of hiding it. I try to focus on work but I spot Roman sitting next to a woman in a bikini who must be Tiffany. I swear she puts her hand on his thigh.

My surveillance is interrupted by a child's voice. "Miss Lifeguard?"

Steven stands by the lifeguard chair, tugging at the string of his swim trunks awkwardly. "Tyler peed in the pool."

Don't tell me this I almost say but stop myself. "I appreciate the update," I tell him. "He shouldn't do that, but we have chemicals that help keep the pool clean."

"I told him he shouldn't!" Steven insists.

"And you're right," I nod. With my sunglasses hiding my gaze I glance at Roman and Tiffany. "Maybe you should talk to Tyler's mom about that."

Steven nods. He waddles over to Roman and his friend. I can't hear the conversation over the splashing and shouting of the pool, but I notice both Tiffany and Roman's face turning red with embarrassment.

Satisfied, I return my attention to the pool just as I hear someone call Tyler's name.

———

There's something I want.

Oh?

Let me know how much money you need

$40.

That's it?

I'm just grabbing a bath bomb.

Why did you send me $200?

Because you deserve it! All the bath bombs :D

and I want photos of you in the bath ;)

There it is. I can manage that.

I think I'll get some oil too for my scales.

Whatever you want dear. You deserve all the
little self care things.

When are you free this weekend? I'm getting
dragged to a bonfire party.

But that sounds fun! I'm going to brunch with
some friends on Sunday and the kids are
back Sunday night.

Damn, the bonfire is Saturday night.

That's okay! I can get a babysitter if you want
to meet during the week.

Maybe just something casual? Movie date?

So it's nice and dark and we can do what we
want?

I was thinking I want to see how jumpy you
are during horror movies.

Well that's rude >:|

But that's not a no

As long as you promise to hold my hand
during the scary parts!

Deal. I'll be sure to send you bathtub pics
when I get home

Perfect ;)

––––––

THE BONFIRE'S popping embers are more comforting
than the booming bass at most college parties. The beach is

packed. Everyone, including me, has a beer in their hands. Goldie sneaks up behind me, one of her claws tapping at my can. "Let me have a sip. I got a shitty IPA."

I give her the beer, not wanting to trade what I think is some sort of lager or an IPA. All the drinks are shoved in a cooler away from the light of the fire. It's like a mini-game, grab a beer and taste to see what you get. Goldie takes a lady-like sip of my beer. A trill noise rises at the back of her throat, her feathers fluffing up.

"You can have it," I offer, not really wanting to get wasted tonight anyway.

"You're the best roommate," she chips.

"Hey!" Jessie whines, walking up with a guy in tow. She pouts at Goldie. "I thought I was the best roommate."

"You're my best friend, not my best roommate."

The guy standing behind Jess grins. He's a complete stranger, but that shit-stirring smile tells me everything I need to know about him. "*Just* best friends huh?"

Jessie elbows him in the ribs. "Shut up, Xander."

Goldie takes a gulp of beer. I can't help but look at my roommates with a new lens. They've been friends forever, but how many love songs have started with friends? I'm sure Sappho wrote a few poems about her dear Nymph friends.

"Just saying, Goldie is gay by default! Fishfolk are the same right?"

I keep quiet, hoping he's asking some other Fishfolk I haven't seen yet. There are a few other monsters besides me and Goldie, some Dragonfolk, I definitely saw a Minotaur wearing a letterman jacket.

"I took this Intro to Earth Species class last semester— I'm premed."

I take it back. I'm too sober for this. I'm about to ask Goldie for the shitty IPA she has somewhere but Xander just keeps talking. Worse yet, he gets closer to me.

"Fishfolk are monosexual, just like Harpies. So you're all gay right?"

I roll my eyes. "Pretty sure you need an intro to Sociology course to answer that one."

"Xander," Goldie chimes in, "Just because I was nice enough to explain all of this to you in high school doesn't mean Lydia has to."

"So you've always been like this?" I deadpan.

Xander chuckles, "Curious? Yeah, always. I asked Jess plenty of questions about you. Had to make sure you were chill before inviting you out. But I hear business majors know how to party."

"Sure," I shrug. "Gotta train for all the open bars at investor parties."

"I'll drink to that!" He pulls an unopened beer from his cargo-pants pocket and tosses it to me.

I'm about to pop the tab when Goldie stops me, guiding my hand so the can is upside down. She gives the round edge a tap, then rips a little hole in the metal with her claw. Okay, so Xander was right, I do know a thing or two about getting wasted at college parties. Without any instruction I bring the punctured can to my lips before ripping the tab. Beer fills my throat so fast I can't even tell what kind it is.

Jessie whoops and Xander joins in. I tilt my head back to get the last of the alcohol out before crushing the can, the crunching of metal a satisfying sound. Xander claps his hands. "Hell yeah! Dope roommate find, Jess."

Instead of responding to him, Jessie grabs my wrist and drags me away from the bonfire. Goldie follows, the three of us stopping in front of the coolers with the rest of the beer. "Sorry about him," Jessie says. "He's my ex-step brother. Kind of unavoidable."

"Has anyone told you your brother has a monster fetish?"

"Yes!" Goldie squawks before pointing at herself. "*Me.* I've told her that. For *years.*"

"He's just… interested in biology," Jessie offers. "You've got to admit, the variation in monster physiology is pretty interesting."

I bump Goldie's hip with my own. "Fine, I'll admit, I didn't know Harpies were monosexual too. Gonna ignore the other stuff, but that's interesting."

"They're all female," Jessie adds with a smile. "So what Xander said is true but—"

"But it's like you said, Lydia, Harpy colonies look at sexuality differently than Humans. You could call a Harpy colony a big lesbian polycule, but no Harpy would call it that."

Jess digs around in the cooler. "Twisted Tea for my favorite feathered friend." She tosses the can to Goldie. "What are you drinking, Lydia?"

I shake my head. "I think I'm alright." The lake is placid in stark contrast to the party surrounding us. "Is anyone going to swim?"

Jessie snorts. "After spending all day at the pool you want to swim?"

"It's not like we get time to *actually* swim," I point out. "And the pool water is gross."

"Lake water isn't?"

Goldie chimes in. "It's better than chemicals on top of BO."

I nod at her in recognition, then head for the water.

Jessie cups her hands around her lips and shouts, "What if you drown?"

That gets the smallest chuckle out of me before I dive into the water, still wearing my shirt and jean shorts. If there wasn't such a large party on the beach I would have gone commando. As it is, the jeans restrain my hips as I rock up and down through the water. It's dark but I can still make out some fish swimming away from me.

When I surface I roll onto my back. The city seems so far away till you look at the sky and realize there are no stars. It's almost midnight and the sky is still a deep blue— blue, not black. Growing up I took for granted my nightly glimpse of constellations.

Not that I *miss* the Midwest. My parents swore that the Great Lakes were just as nice as the ocean proper. One of the first things I did when I wasn't swamped with classes was visit the shore. The Great Lakes raised me, but nothing can compare to the power and vastness of the Atlantic.

Maybe if I can't land a good enough internship after college, I can run away to grad school out West. Get a taste of both oceans.

I sit up, treading water and getting a sense of where I am. The closest shoreline leads right up into someone's backyard. Which I hadn't considered when I left the party. Spinning around in the dark I struggle to find the beach.

A light shines in the corner of my eye. The porch lights of the nearest house have turned on. At this hour I expect to see a dog or some raccoon scurry past. Instead, a figure stands at the porch's edge. It's like something out of a high school English book I never bothered to read; this captivating figure looking out over the water at the back of their lavish mansion.

Except the longer I look, the more familiar the figure is. I get low in the water, everything below my eyes submerged, and swim forward. There's a decent amount of yard between the lake's edge and the porch, but still I'm certain I know the woman. Hard not to remember that body.

Steph is wearing a silky robe with a pattern I can't quite make out. Not that florals or intricate designs can hold my attention when their canvas is much more interesting. My feet find the lake floor and I start walking, not bothering to hide myself.

Steph spots me with a jump, grabbing her chest and then laughing. "Oh gosh— you're— oh I shouldn't say that."

"Say what?" The water is up to my waist now, shirt clinging to my gills.

Steph steps off of her porch and into the yard, her feet bare but the yard meticulous and thick with trimmed grass. "You… reminded me of this old movie, black and white, handsome monsters."

"Handsome?"

"Well, not as handsome as you. Nowhere near as pretty."

We're face to face now. Me dripping with lake water, no doubt a bit of pond scum in my hair and wet denim covering ass. While she looks like she's about to relax with some wine and reality TV. Though the way she looks at me it's like I'm dripping with diamonds, whatever plans she had flung far out the window.

"If you wanted to see me, you should have just texted."

"It's my turn to be terrible. I wasn't planning on seeing you. There's a party on the lake…" As I explain, I look past her at the house. It's three stories tall, the porch is made of puddingstone. The windows on the first floor are large enough that I can clearly see the living room. Looking up, one of the second stories has a balcony.

Any less would be a waste of a lakefront property I guess.

Steph blinks. "So you're trespassing?" She winks. "I'll have to book you myself."

"You'll never take me alive," I grin.

"Do you want to come in and dry off? I guess you'll just get wet again…" She points back at the lake. "Would you like a drink?"

"I'm the DD for my roommates," I explain. It's funny how insistent she's being. It kind of reminds me of a mom, but I know this goes beyond average hospitality. "Do you have tea?"

She smiles and I was wrong about not seeing any stars tonight. Her eyes sparkle as she tells me "I've got plenty."

Inside I'm greeted with marble floors then say hello to matching marble countertops in the kitchen. My wet feet slap against the floor. I know her kids are with their dad so it should be just the two of us. While Steph fiddles with an electric kettle I get a better look at her robe.

The pattern is kind of floral. At first I think they're vines but looking closer and noticing the white accents are pearls, I recognize macrocystis seaweed on a dark blue background. "Wow," I say without thinking.

Steph glances over her shoulder.

"That's a nice robe."

"Down girl," she giggles. "At least have a drink with me first."

"I should have been more specific, that's an expensive robe. I recognize the fabric." Though for the life of me I can't remember the designer. Some couture house my ex was obsessed with.

Steph's cheeks are pink. She quickly grabs a box and shoves it in my face. Dozens of different tea bags all lined up, organized by color. "I don't have any loose leaf." She says, a hint of embarrassment in her voice. I'm not sure if it's because I recognized that her robe is half a semester's tuition or if it's because she only has bagged tea.

I peer past the box and find her face is even redder than before. Because of me? I grab a tea bag, not really thirsty. At least not that sort of thirsty.

Stephanie returns the tea to the counter and I follow. When she turns back around I pin her to the counter with my hips. Steph hisses. "You're so cold."

I bat my eyelashes, innocently. "Can't you warm me up?" I push a streak of grey behind her ear. "Better than the tea I bet."

Steph takes a shaky breath, her pupils fully dilated.

"No comeback? You know I like when you flirt with me, don't you?"

She nods, but says "It takes a bit of getting used to. I realized maybe I wasn't so obvious before…"

"We couldn't really be obvious at the club…" *In front of your kids* I think but don't dare say.

The kettle screams and Steph swiftly grabs me a mug. I don't want to be rude so I accept the tea. It does smell good, whatever it is.

"I don't want to keep you from the party." It's like she's already forgotten our flirting.

"I want you to keep me," I assure her. "It's a bunch of my roommates' friends. They're probably fine but I'd much rather hang out with you."

"Your roommates' friends aren't your friends?" She wanders out of the kitchen and I follow, the two of us settling into the living room. Steph puts a blanket down over the leather couch, my jeans no longer soaking but still a bit damp.

"It's just a summer situation. I've only known them for a few weeks."

"Oh, I thought they might be friends from college." She pulls her knees to her chest. "Do you know anyone from around here?"

"Nope. Most of my college friends have internships in the city or went back home."

Steph tits her head thoughtfully. "You sound bitter."

I choke on my tea.

"Sorry— that was Stephanie talking."

I clear my throat but my voice is still a touch strained. "What?"

"Stephanie does market analysis for a fortune five hundred company. Steph is a mom who likes to make green tea shots for her mommy friends on the weekends."

My mug feels heavier now. Certainly a lot heavier than a green tea shot. Why didn't she offer me that? Right, DD, responsible roommate.

"Well… Stephanie is right," I admit. I abandon my teacup on a nearby end table. Her hand cups my cheek, thumb fingering a scale. "I am bitter. Not as bitter as I was a few months ago…"

"A little bitterness is good, there's a reason they add them to good whiskey." Her robe does little to cover her curves. If anything the satin makes it more apparent, clinging to her hips and breasts and shimmering like dragonfly wings. Staring is an understatement. She's walking art right before me. Mona Lisa couldn't hold a candle to her.

I swallow hard. "I'll have to try one of your drinks sometime."

She pulls her hand from my cheek then trails it down her collar, letting those bubblegum pink fingernails push aside some fabric, showing off more of her breasts. My tongue traces along my teeth, desperate to have her nipple between my lips once more.

"Still thirsty?" Before I can respond she sits in my lap. She strokes my cheek, looking at me with a sort of affection I'm not used to. It's not pure lust— no it's far softer, more comforting. She pushes back the satin resting on her shoulders, exposing her chest fully. Again, she asks, "are you thirsty, dear?"

I dive face first into her bosom, letting her mounds warm my cheeks before kissing the roundest parts. Finally I find her nipple and take it into my mouth, sucking softly. "There, take all you need from mommy."

I suck harder, letting my teeth graze her nipple. She lets out a sharp gasp before growing, "God, you're so needy." She strokes my hair. "I love it…"

With a pop I abandon one breast and let my mouth explore the other. My hand teases her wet, erect nipple. Her other nipple is already hard, and I take it as a complement. "Good girl," she breathes. "So good for mommy." Stephanie rubs her thighs together.

There's a battle in my brain, a war between having her ride my fingers or letting her sit on my face. Not that I can't do both. Make her cum on my fingers before she rides my tongue. My fantasy of filling her with my pearl-like eggs is just a whisper, but it's there.

Before I can settle on a battle plan, Stephanie pulls away. I'm ready to beg for her to get back in my lap when she drops a pillow to the floor before falling to her knees in front of me. Her brown eyes sparkle, lips parted in a pout that makes her look like the centerfold of a dirty magazine. I tug off my bottoms without thinking. The denim sticks to my skin and it's a bigger battle than it should be. Meanwhile my tentacles writhe, as if waving to Steph, their new favorite person.

Once I'm pantless and sitting back on the couch she takes one tentacle in her mouth, the rest caressing her cheeks and chin. I watch in awe as she bobs her head, taking more and more of me in her mouth.

I'm not sure how to tell her… Not sure I want to.

But then she pulls back and cocks her head, the tip of one of my tentacles bushing against her bottom lip. "Is that good?"

I bite my lip. "I can't… really feel it."

"Oh."

"But it's hot," I promise her.

Steph looks at my tentacles with new confusion. "They aren't erogenous?"

"They're practical," I explain. "I'm… Not sure how much you want to hear."

Steph puts her hand out, letting the tentacles play with her fingers, wrapping around them, suctioning to her fingertips. "I want to know everything," she tells me, not taking her eyes off the writhing bundle of flesh and suction cups.

"When I spawn, lay eggs, the tentacles help put them where they need to go. Some monsters have ovipositors that do that for them. Fishfolk have tentacles."

"Oh." Steph kisses the backside of a tentacle. "How practical…"

Not wanting her to stop doting on the appendage, I stroke her hair. "I did like that. You taking them in your mouth. I might not feel it but it *looks* hot."

That's all the encouragement she needs to take not one, but two of my tentacles in her mouth. Her head bobs, lewd sucking noises filling the room. One tentacle tries to worm its way past her lips, as if jealous it's not exploring her mouth.

"Loosen your lips."

Her mouth relaxes and the tentacle dives in her mouth—Steph making a little *murp* sound before another tentacle fills her. I'm mesmerized as more and more of my tentacles explore her mouth, her cheeks bulging with writhing tentacles. Her eyes start to water but she doesn't pull back.

"You look so beautiful, Steph," I breathe.

Steph manages a little sound, loosening her jaw to let the tentacles have free rein of her mouth.

"Since you're being so good, why don't you touch yourself?"

Another muffled sound before she slips a hand between her thighs.

"Fill yourself with your fingers, that's it, you're so good to me you deserve to cum while choking on me."

A single tear appears at the edge of her pretty eye and I reach down to wipe it away. Now I just appreciate the squelching noises of her fingers pumping in and out of her cunt, the slick sliding in and out of my tentacles as they fuck her mouth. I might not be able to feel her tongue or the back of her throat but fuck if it isn't hot watching her choke on me.

"Mommy feel good?" I coo and Steph barely manages a nod. "Like choking on me?" I take the back of her head and push her forward, letting my tentacles push past her cheeks and down her throat. Steph's eyes roll back. Past her head I see her ass bounce as she grinds against her fingers. "Fuck Steph, I don't know where to look, your ass your your pretty mouth."

She gags but doesn't try and pull away. So diligent, maybe even a bit stubborn about taking it like the best mom on the slutty PTA. Drool drips past her lips practically making a puddle on the floor. She's completely wracked with pleasure, but I'm clear headed enough to keep talking.

"You should see yourself right now, how dull your eyes are, just so full of my tentacles you can't think about anything else. I'd love to watch your pussy be full of my tentacles next. You'd like that wouldn't you? Getting so full you can't stand without spilling my spawn?"

A strained whimper fills the room and I know she's finished on her fingers. Grabbing a handful of her dark hair I pull her back off my tentacles but they still reach for her. Steph gasps for breath past swollen lips. One tentacle manages to wrap itself around the edge of her mouth, tugging at it. I giggle, "Aw they love you mommy."

She manages to speak despite half her mouth being pulled in one direction. "Lydia..."

"There are so many things I want to do to you..." Her eyes are still glassy. "But maybe one new thing at a time..."

"Lydia..." She repeats and I wonder if she's heard a single thing I've said.

My own hand dips between my thighs, my tentacles paying it no mind. Two fingers slip inside me with ease. When I pull them back they're glistening with pearly white slick. I offer my fingers to Steph who greedily takes them in her mouth and moans.

"Do I taste good?" I ask before pulling my fingers back but Steph wraps her lips and tongue tight around them, not wanting them gone. Still I manage to rear my hand away from her lips with a little popping sound.

Steph swallows before responding. "You taste... salty. But sweet." Her lips still red from being fucked stretch into a smile. "You remind me of saltwater taffy."

"That's a new one."

She starts to stand and I lean forward to catch her in case she falls but she just settles back in my lap. Her lips find mine and they are so warm, plump, and do in fact taste faintly of salt. Her tongue is even saltier and I suck on it, Steph responding with a moan into my mouth. I grab her ass, working it up and down. There's so much of her to grab. To tease and play with.

When she pulls away, I can already tell what she's about to ask me. "Next time… do you want to do the egg thing?"

I shouldn't laugh but I do. Even worse it's an undignified snort. "Sorry, I've never heard it called the egg thing."

"Well, what do you call it?"

I shrug to try and make the word less daunting, "Breeding."

Steph's mouth falls open. "Oh. That's… I'm sorry I didn't realize you could get me pregnant."

It's my turn to be stumped. "I don't think I can? The eggs are pretty finicky. They need a very specific environment to gestate. I love your cunt, but I don't think it's capable of that."

Steph sighs with relief. "Okay. So we can still do it?"

Her eagerness is such a turn on, but her questions have me thinking less than horny thoughts. "I'll do some research to be sure." I take her hand, "You should research things too. Make sure it'll be something you're into." She opens her mouth and I shut her up with a kiss. "For me, do some research." I whisper against her lips. "Watch some videos. Tell me how you like it."

She bites her lip, looking so demure despite… despite everything leading up to this point. Up close like this I see her crows feet plainly, notice her roots are lighter than the rest of her hair, I can fairly smell my salt on her breath.

She is so far from innocent, but fuck I want to corrupt her more.

I stand, so sudden my head spins but I manage to stay upright. "I should head back."

Steph's voice jumps an octave. "Right," She clears her throat. "Designated drivers. That's nice of you…"

"I promise, next time won't be so…" My head bobbles side to side. "Fuckboy."

Steph rests her chin in her hand. "Maybe that's just my type."

"Oof," I place my hand over my heart as I back away. "Next time we'll do cuddles and plenty of aftercare— swear on my life."

She relaxes, sultry eyes and a smirk that makes me weak all over again. "Next time," she agrees. "You owe me a movie date."

I nod. "Just tell me when you get a babysitter and I'll make it work."

Once I'm on the back porch I sprint to the lake. Diving into the water I swim, not sure where I'm going but aware I'm weak and willing to fall on my knees between Steph's legs and stay over.

Abandoning my drunk roommates is not bestie behavior.

When I surface I'm at the center of the lake. It takes some looking around but I spot faint lights and movement in the distance. I swim that way and sure enough, I find myself back at the beach. A couple guys in snapbacks stare at me as I exit the water. Normally I wouldn't give them a second thought, but Steph comparing me to those old movie monsters gets me curious. The whites of their eyes catch moonlight, one of them with their mouth hanging open like a wall-mounted bass.

I can't help myself. "Any one of you seen Goldie?" I give them a mean glare like they're responsible for me losing track of my roommate.

The slack jawed one shuts his mouth but is unhelpful. Another one grunts and gestures in a direction with his solo cup. Helpful and completely useless all at once. No wonder so many Fishfolk used to eat guys like that.

Wandering through the groups of people I eventually spot

familiar wings from behind a tree. "Goldie!" No response. I get closer. "Hey, Goldie have you seen Jessie?"

Jessie pops out from behind the tree first, swaying a little. Figures they'd be together.

"Hey you guys want to head out? No offense Jessie but I'm not sure this is my scene."

"Whatda mean?" She blinks slowly. "Rich kids drinking away dada's money aren't your best-ees?"

"No. Are you drunk?"

Goldie finally comes out, her face flush. "There was a keg–"

"Kegstand!"

Well at least it sounds like all three of us had a good time. "Sorry I missed it. You want to head home?"

"Yeah," Jessie pushes her hair back. "Good idea. Ew but you're wet."

Goldie blows air past her lips. "Your car reeks of chlorine."

"And we have towels in the trunk, remember?"

Jessie hums and starts meandering towards the car. As we walk I pull Goldie aside. "She's not gonna puke is she?"

"N-no she'll be fine." Goldie eyes the ground.

"Are you good?"

"Rich kids aren't really my besties either."

I nod. Maybe this night wasn't the best for everyone. Not that I have any right to complain.

Goldie sits in the back with Jessie while I play chauffeur. Goldie helps guide me out of town and once we hit the highway I just follow the familiar exits. I'm shocked Jessie is still awake when we get back to the apartment. "Thaaaanksss Liddds."

"Never call me Lids again and I'd be DD whenever you want."

CHAPTER
Seven

IT'S a short walk from the bathroom to the front door but my roommates catch me anyway. "You look nice," Jessie comments.

I make a casual glance at my outfit, a black flannel overtop a wife pleaser with a barbed wire heart. My jean shorts are black as well, fall just above the knee, and the nicest pair I own. As if anyone can tell the difference between dress-jean-shorts and cruddy-jean-shorts. Except Jessie seems to have noticed.

The feathers around Goldie's neck bristle. "Are you wearing makeup?"

"Lipgloss barely counts." I wonder if Goldie can smell that it's green tea flavored. Steph gave me so much liquid to spend at the fancy bath store I ended up buying things I normally wouldn't.

Jessie and Goldie look at each other and I'm reminded they've known each other for years. They just have that telepathic look in their eyes like they're having a whole conversation without me. Instead of pointing this out, I take this as my opportunity to escape.

Steph is already waiting for me downstairs in her SUV. The windows have a dark tint so I can't see her driving, but my heart races anyway. I hop into the front seat and waste no time giving her a kiss. When I pull away she whispers, "Wait," and catches my lips again.

This time she's the one who pulls away, licking her lips. "You taste like matcha."

"Thoughts?"

She starts driving, humming to herself as she thinks. "I'm not sure I love a salty matcha."

"Wow."

"Caramel would be nice!" She offers. "But I'm not picky."

"I don't believe that for a second."

Steph just giggles to herself as she merges onto the highway. I'm not completely sure where we're going besides the fact it's a movie theater. There are a whole bunch, from the big named chains to IMAX theaters to luxury theater experiences. All I care about is a dark room with enough bass to drown us out. I've never fooled around in a movie theater. It feels like such a teenage thing to do and teenage me wasn't very popular with the ladies. I guess the fact I was standing in a glass closet didn't make me all that appealing.

At first I think we're going to Newark of all places but we cross a bridge and end up in Jersey City. "I thought we could go for a walk along the waterfront after the movie," Steph explains.

"Smart." It would be kind of a waste to sit and fool around in the dark all night. Out the window it's like we're back in New York, though the streets remind me more of Williamsburg or the Heights. Not nearly as crowded or bougie as Soho, but still packed full of small shops bursting with personality. That is till we pull into a mall parking lot.

"What is with this state and malls?" I grumble.

Steph shrugs. "Taking advantage of sales tax? I'm not

sure, but we sure do have a lot of them." As soon as we're both out of the car she takes my hand. She's wearing a white blouse and a comfortable looking pair of jeans. It's impossible to compare them to the emerald dress she wore on our last date but she still looks great. Effortless.

I feel a little silly bothering with lipgloss.

Inside the mall we see the theater marquee and Steph squeezes my hand. "Do we really have to see a horror movie?"

"Well now we *really* have to."

Steph makes a face that I've only ever seen her kid's before; a pouting frown with her nose all scrunched up.

"Didn't you say the Creature from the Black Lagoon is handsome? Slashers don't do it for you?"

"They all wear masks," she points out. "The Creature is a unique beauty."

As she says it, I catch sight of a tall woman around my age standing with a group of other girls. Even with the gaggle of girls I can't take my eyes off her. Her skin is a peachy tan like a conch shell. While she's not especially curvy her features are striking, large eyes and lips with high cheekbones and a tight jaw. All of it is perhaps overshadowed by her thick turquoise hair that floats around her like she's submerged in water.

My ex hasn't noticed me yet and I silently pray she doesn't.

Steph and I stand in line for tickets. "Whatever you want to watch," I fold, as if that will make the line move faster "I was just teasing about the horror movie..."

Steph lifts a brow. "I know. I thought it was funny." She purses her lips. "Let's see..." As she studies the movie posters I shift us around so she's standing in-between me and my ex. Sure, I'm a good inch or two taller than Steph but why would Ari look twice at Steph? Other than the obvious, she's an attractive woman wearing jeans that make her ass look amazing.

When we get up to the counter I don't even hear what movie Steph has picked out. The ocean roars in my ears and I worry my palm is getting sweaty. Despite everything we're still holding hands. As soon as Steph has the tickets in her hands I drag her past the concessions and to the movie proper. "That stuff is always such a rip," I tell her.

"Oh it's okay–" She insists but doesn't tug me back in the direction of the overpriced popcorn and sweets. "The theater is that way," she points and I lead.

Just before we turn the corner I make the mistake of looking back, like some sailor already homesick though the shore is in sight. Ari and I lock eyes for a second– no, less than a second, before the wall blocks us.

We settle in our seats and I take a deep breath. The trailers have already started but Steph's eyes are on me. I wait for a trailer to end before acknowledging her. "That one looks interesting."

Steph tilts her head like a confused puppy but doesn't say anything. The churning waves in my ears have died down. Now it's just the loud dialogue from the trailer. I lean in to whisper right in Steph's ear. "Is it too early to start making out?"

"Save that for the gory scenes," she says.

The movie has way more jump-scares than blood or guts but they get Steph every time. With every loud sting from the soundtrack she does a little hop in her seat, sucking in air before exhaling and touching her heart. I bite the inside of my lip to suppress my laughter.

We came in late so I didn't get a chance to scope out the theater. Whenever the screen is bright enough I try to see who all is nearby. Our row is pretty empty but there is a couple in the row behind us. Not right behind us but close enough they might notice us getting handsy. Especially since the movie is so boring.

Eventually I lean over and start kissing Steph's neck. She

ignores me, but I can feel the muscles in her neck flex beneath my lips. My hand finds her thigh, then my fingertips slip beneath her blouse, pinching the round of her stomach. Steph wriggles in her seat. My hand travels farther up her torso till I can palm her breasts over her bra. Still she ignores me, her eyes on the screen, but I don't hate this.

I squeeze her. Nip at her neck. Finally when I suck at her collar hard enough to leave a mark she grabs me by the back of my head and pulls me to her lips. I smile against her, feeling accomplished. We kiss for a while, Steph running her hand up and down my flat chest. My thighs rub together and I really do feel like a teenager getting off from her touch, from the tip of her tongue against mine.

Someone coughs and Steph and I pull away, our hands now at our sides. We sit there, both of us as small as possible. The familiar sound of Steph trying and failing to stifle a giggle, makes me laugh right as the murderer is getting gutted by a pair of hedge clippers.

I have no clue what this movie is even about. I cover Steph's eyes as more and more guts fill the screen. She smiles, holds my wrist keeping my hand in place for the rest of the movie.

When the lights come up I remove my hand from her face. "That was a terrible movie," she tells me. "I don't think it would have made sense even if I was paying attention."

"The effects were good," I argue.

Steph sticks out her tongue and scrunches her nose.

"See? That's how you know it was good. Or at least passable."

"Maybe it's a good thing we didn't get any food. It would have just made me sick."

I nod. "Not to mention the butter in unwanted places."

My lips are still tingling as we exit the theater and I've completely forgotten about Ari. At this point I'm not even completely sure it was her. There are plenty of tall women with bright blue hair in the world. The thought is comforting only for a moment.

Steph's mouth falls open as we pass the mall food court. "Oh wow."

I follow her eyes, stopping at a table brimming with beautiful, tall, thin women. Upon closer inspection most of them have feathers and scales. Not nearly as many as Goldie or I, but they're there. Some Fishfolk look more Human than others, their more fishy features only coming out when they're in the water. Mermaids are a good example.

Ari, who is looking at me with a bored expression, is the perfect example.

"They must be models," Steph breathes. Her mouth hangs open and her eyes are wide like a kid in a candy store.

"I think they're just fashion students." Which is absolutely something you can just tell by looking at people and not me letting on that I know who these women are.

Steph grabs my wrist. "Oh, one of them is walking this way."

I don't bother looking, knowing damn well who it is. I can hear waves crashing against rocks but I stay focused on Steph. Her cheeks are starting to turn pink and I shake my head. "I can't believe I get to witness your first gay panic."

That snaps her out of it. *"First?"*

"I thought that was you…" A smokey voice sings. Steph and I both look at Ari standing in front of us with her hands on her hips. Her top is tight with just the very bottom of her very flat stomach poking out. Her skirt is either vintage or designed to look two decades too old. It's like she's heading to a concert and not some mall in Jersey City. "Who's your friend, Lydia?" She flutters her eyelashes slowly, like a predator noticing prey.

Steph's voice is strained. "You two know each other?"

Fuck. No point in beating around the bush. "Ari is my ex."

Ari pops her hip, one hand falling to her side. "Uh, wow, rude. I'm so much more than that." She flashes Steph a smile, her teeth as white as pearls or bones after they've had all the meat stripped away. Ari might look harmless but historically, Fishfolk who look like her have been deadly predators. There's a reason she's so alluring and it has nothing to do with attracting a mate. Despite what poor sailors might think.

"Hi, I'm Ari. Lydia and I go to NYU together." She pushes her natural blue hair behind her ear. "How do you two know each other?"

Of course she'd ask that. It's an innocent enough question. But I know that smile, recognize the way Ari scans Steph. She's already decided if Steph is worth her time, but why not play with her food a little?

Steph blinks. "We're… um…"

I'm not sure if Steph is just struggling because there's a beautiful woman in front of her or if she really doesn't have a cover for that question. I'm not sure I have a cover. *We just meet up once a week to hold hands in public, totally normal and not sexual stuff here!*

"Lydia," Ari wines. "Don't leave your friend on dry land. What's the story? Don't tell me you're *dating* again? What am I? Chum?" She starts to laugh but it's short and hollow, making me feel like a cinderblock is pulling me down to the ocean depths.

It's also kind of hot. Despite everything, Ari's mean girl glance still does something to me.

"You broke up with me," I stammer. My lips twitch but no words come out. Ari wraps a strand of blue around a perfectly manicured finger with oversized seashell charms. At least I know *she's* not seeing anyone. Despite appearances, she's far from a pillow princess.

Steph finds her voice again. "Lydia never mentioned her

ex. It's nice to meet you." She sounds kind but not overly sweet. "Do you live around here?"

Ari makes a disgusted noise at the back of her throat. "As if. We're just passing through. Pop up event in the Power House district. Guess they couldn't find anyone willing to host in Tribeca." She rolls her eyes.

"Well that sounds fun. I'm Stephanie, by the way."

I want to grab her shoulders, shake and shout, *do not speak to the siren!* But there's no real point in it now.

It's striking how different they are. Physically, Ari is a bit taller than me with zero curves so it's easy to see why Steph thought she was a model. Meanwhile Steph is short and round, warm and inviting. Personality wise they're opposites too. When Steph's kindness made my heart race, it was a surprise. I'd always been drawn to mean girls— the challenge they brought. I'd flirted with Ari for months before she gave me the time of day. It felt so good when she finally kissed me. But not any better than Steph's lips…

Ari grins. "Stephanie? So you two are…"

"Business partners." She laughs. "Or hopeful ones. When I was Lydia's age I would have loved a mentor, so I'm paying that forward."

"Cute." Ari says like someone's shoved their geriatric purse dog in her face. "You two have fun with that." With that she leaves, hair and skirt flowing behind her like she's on a damn catwalk. She rejoins her friends. Some words are exchanged before they all roar with laughter.

Steph's hand on my lower back makes me jump. "You alright? Maybe we should get some fresh air. There's a park nearby."

We walk along the waterfront, New York's skyline like a light show before us. Not that anything can compete with the view from Steph's office. Being so close to the water is nice, lights and building silhouettes reflecting off the water's surface. It almost makes me forget this is the Hudson and I'd rather eat my own scales than dive into its murky depths.

The concrete gives way to an open green space, the majority of it taken up by a playground that could fit in at an amusement park. There are so many things to climb and swing on. There's even a splash pad, though the water is turned off, with tall fountains shaped like mushrooms. "This is nice," I breathe.

Steph laughs. "New Jersey is actually pretty nice if you know where to go." She leads me to the swings. We're the only people partaking in the playground. Couples and other groups walk past us on spiraling walkways. I sit and hold myself. Steph wastes no time pumping her legs and getting up in the air.

"Do you want to talk about what happened?"

She moves like a pendulum which should make this whole conversation harder, but the air of whimsey makes it all feel less serious. Still I huff, "What is there to talk about?"

Steph drags her feet in the wood chips and slows down. "You looked pretty shell shocked when we ran into Ari. I wasn't sure if you wanted to… elaborate?" She purses her lips. "Maybe you're right and there isn't anything to talk about. You would know."

I let go of my torso and grab the swing chains, pumping my legs. "We broke up really suddenly. Or, it was sudden for me. I guess that was part of the problem." I realize I'm not making much sense but Steph nods anyway. "There was this internship, super competitive but I thought I had a really good shot. Like they called just a few hours after my first interview and wanted me to come in for a second one. Really fast response times."

"That's not normative," Steph agrees. "Sounds like they didn't want you snatched up by anyone else."

I pump my legs harder, wind wiping in my ears. "I didn't

want to go with anyone else. So I got kinda obsessed. Spent a lot of time in mock interviews, talking with my professors and alums for tips– they even invited me to an event and–" I leg my legs dangle, shoes dragging across the ground. When I stop moving I finish my thought. But it's more a confession. "The event was on Ari's birthday. I still showed up to her party but super late and I know she was pissed off but I told her we'd have all summer together."

I rest my cheek against the swing chain. "I got to the final round of interviews but they picked someone else. I cried a bunch. When I was done sobbing out another ocean– Ari broke up with me."

"Oh!" Steph leaps forward, placing her hand on my thigh. "Lydia, sweetie, I'm so sorry."

I shake my head but my eyes feel so dry, the way they always do right before I start crying. "Don't be. I should have had a backup, maybe reflected, prioritized…"

"Your future should be your priority," Steph's expression is stern. "I don't think you did anything wrong. Did Ari tell you she needed you at her party?"

"No, but she pouted about it. I should have, I don't know, left the company event earlier or tried to do something nice for her, just the two of us."

Steph chews her bottom lip. "Maybe… I'm still learning how to balance all of that," she admits.

"It doesn't really matter now." I slump my shoulders. "The messiest part was all my friends telling me they never really liked her. Everyone says she's too much of a mean girl."

"I gathered that."

"So we're never getting back together. And I'm never going to try and intern at that company again." I look forward, glaring at the city skyline.

"Well–" Steph shuts her mouth, swallowing whatever words she was about to say. "There are plenty of great companies you could intern at, but it does sound like this place wanted you."

I lift a brow. "You think I should still try and work at the place that rejected me?"

"Egos serve no one in this line of work Lydia. Who knows, maybe you got passed over by the perfect candidate or maybe an investor's kid. Would you really tell them no if they offered you a spot?"

"I haven't thought about it. To be honest I haven't thought about an adult job since I got rejected. Lifeguarding is easier to focus on."

Steph surprises me with a laugh. "Having people's lives in your hands is less stressful than spreadsheets?" She pats my knee, still chuckling to herself. "I promise you, one missed internship won't ruin your career."

"But three summers of lifeguarding won't help it."

Steph rolls her eyes. "You handle children, drunks, safety, and I don't even want to know what goes into keeping that water considered legally clean. You're more prepared for the corporate world than most graduates. I understand practical skills don't turn heads the same as corporation names but you frame your skills right...." She pauses and I recognize that soft glint in her eyes that tells me she's thinking.

"Have you ever gone to an auction?" She asks.

"Like... can I get 350 for the couch someone probably died on?"

Steph smiles. "No, lots of corporations hold auctions for their shareholders and employees. It's a great way to make connections. And watch drunk people pay too much for Broadway tickets."

"Sounds more like dinner and a show."

Her smile blooms. "Come with me. I usually skip them but my company is holding one in August. Quite a few partners will be there. I'll introduce you to some people."

I hesitate. Which isn't like me. Of course I want to drink

and schmooze with rich folks. That's the dream. "How would you introduce me?"

"This is Lydia," she gestures to me, "She's a very promising student at NYU and the most level headed person I've had the pleasure of meeting. I'd make her my assistant if I didn't think it's a waste of her skills."

I blink. "You'd make me your assistant?" My palm catches my cheek. It's warming up and I wonder if Steph notices in the dark.

"I wouldn't get any work done with you in the office, dear. But they don't have to know that little tidbit. Everything else is true."

I consider asking her why. Why me? Why are you doing this? Why not anyone else? Steph could just fuck me and buy me fancy meals and I'd be happy. Who wouldn't be? Instead she's offering me so much more. Maybe her goal from the start hasn't been to get me out of my swimsuit, but to get me into a boardroom.

It's been a while since my tentacles have gone so wild for something so mundane and I'm glad my jeans keep everything in place. "I want to go," I tell her. "I'll need a new suit."

Steph brings her hands together like she's about to pray and makes tiny little golf claps.

"But first," I stand up. "I'm hungry. Think we can get anything to eat at this hour?"

"In the shadow of the city that never sleeps? Oh dear, we can get anything we want."

"But to-go." I glance back at the waterfront, sparkling with neon lights. "I want to sit out here for a bit and appreciate the view."

"Of course," Steph agrees. "Anything for you."

———

IT'S one in the morning by the time I sneak back into the apartment. Not that I need to sneak when I'm twenty-one. Or so I thought. I've taken two steps inside when the lights turn on, blinding me.

"Where have you been?" I recognize Jessie's voice, blinking rapidly to adjust to the light. She stands there with her arms crossed. Goldie is right next to her, looking nowhere near as serious.

"Don't you have work in the morning?" Goldie yawns. "Because I do."

"Like you two haven't gone to an 8AM class hung over and still wearing the outfit you partied in." I head for the bathroom, ready to just slip into the tub and sleep what little I can before work. Jessie and Goldie follow me, their shoulders bumping together in the cramped hallway.

"Seriously Lydia, we got worried." Goldie drones, blinking slowly like it takes effort to keep her eyes open.

"Yeah!" Jessie agrees. "You didn't tell us anything about where you went. That's bad girl code."

My hand is on the doorknob ready to shut them out but I stop myself. They aren't nagging me. If I hadn't come home, if I'd slept over with Steph, what would they have done? It's better to have roommates who care than ones that wouldn't bat an eye if you disappeared. "I'm sorry. I went out with a friend is all. Next time I'll tell you where I'm going."

"We just want you to be safe," Jessie explains.

Goldie yawns and rests her cheek on Jessie's shoulder. "She gets it. Let's all go to bed." Goldie doesn't move towards the balcony. Instead Jessie wraps an arm around her waist and leads her to her room.

I lift a brow. "You two going to share a bed?"

Jessie glances over her shoulder and shrugs. "We've slept over dozens of times. It's not weird."

"Never said it was." I swear Goldie nuzzles into Jessie's neck. It's far too late to ask questions. Besides, platonic cuddling sounds nice. "Goodnight." I shut the door and run the bath before taking off my clothes.

Right before I head to bed I get a text from Steph.

Home safe. Goodnight dear.

I'm jealous now of Goldie and Jessie, all tangled up in each other in the next room. Platonic or otherwise.

CHAPTER
Eight

I'm doing a drug store run, sunscreen and hair ties and stuff.

Okay! <3 Make sure you get yourself something fun too

At the drug store? Guess I could get booze.

Or one of those vibrators

Funny you mention toys... I've been doing research like you asked.

Such a good student. You find any videos you like?

It took some digging but yes. I want to show them to you.

In person.

It's a date.

None of the videos are as nice as the bathtub photos you sent me.

I wish I could get them framed.

Where would you even hang those?

My office of course.

You're a dirty old woman.

And what does that make you my little
Guppy?

MILF bait?

There we go ;)

————

GREY CLOUDS OVERHEAD keep the pool patrons away.
I listen for thunder and pray for lightning so we can close up
and go home. All this overcast is a big show for mother
nature. Not even a single raindrop.

Steph and I are meeting tonight. The kids are with Roman
so it will be just the two of us. There's nothing better to do
right now than daydream. But I know where my mind will
wander and I don't want to soak through my bathing suit.
Even if I've got on modesty shorts now.

I climb down from the lifeguard chair and over to the
snack shack. "Carl, can I get a smoothie?" We get a discount
on food and drinks. Discount, not free, which is a rip-off but I
admit, I don't have the guts to tell Lord Unnith that.

Carl doesn't respond. I ring the order bell. Still nothing. I
tap the bell like an impatient child. Still nothing. "Oh come
on." I grumble. If Carl isn't at his post why should I be at
mine? I prop up the pool closed sign and head inside. There's
bound to be something in the fridge I can steal.

I'm not paying any attention to my surroundings when
Carl appears out of thin air. He spots me with his single eye

and jumps. "Fuck–" he catches himself. "Okay, okay, what's up?"

Weird. Since when is Carl jumpy?

Now I *am* paying attention. His polo shirt buttons are undone. His hair is a bit messy and his one eye is red around the edges. My eyes narrow as I try to better size him up, but the biggest clue isn't on Carl. It's behind him. Lord Unnith's office.

"Did Lord Unnith chew you out or something? You look wiped."

Carl runs his fingers through his hair. "Uh, no– seriously, what do you need?" He walks toward me, trying to lead me away from the Lord's office.

I let him usher me out like a bouncer, but with a caveat. "I want a smoothie."

Carl rolls his big eye and it's a wonder he doesn't get dizzy from it.

"Come on, It's so dead out there Carl." He must be as bored as I am. Or was before Lord Unnith called him into his office.

"That doesn't mean you can leave your post."

We're on the pool deck now. "Let me get this straight. You can leave your post to go chit-chat with the boss but I can't leave mine to go find you?"

"Chit-chatting," he scoffs. He enters through the side door of the Snack Shack and heads straight for the freezer, grabbing frozen fruit.

"If you weren't talking and he wasn't yelling then what were you two doing..." My eyes narrow, "Alone..."

Carl is too focused on measuring milk to notice. I focus in on his neck, pale and out in the open with his collar so loose. If he'd bothered to button it I would have never noticed the purple and red splotch just below his collar. It reminds me of a barnacle.

The roar of the blender pulls me away, but Carl has caught

me staring. He gives me a dead eyed stare with a scowling brow. With no one around to hear us, I shout over the blender. "Nice hickey."

Carl shuts off the blender. He clenches his jaw and keeps staring at me. I just snag my wallet and place the money for the smoothie on the counter. He scoffs, throwing his head back dramatically, and pours me my drink.

"Thank you," I take the smoothie and take a long drink.

"Don't tell anyone okay. Especially Jess."

"That you get dick? Yeah I'll keep that to myself."

Carl slams a hand on the counter. "I mean it Lydia, don't tell anyone shit."

"It's a hickey, Carl. I'm–" I almost say I'm surprised I don't have any, what with how touchy Steph and I have been that summer, but I stop myself. "Everyone gets them."

His expression softens. "You… don't realize." He pinches the bridge of his nose.

It's embarrassing how long it takes me to figure out what he's getting at– all the obvious tells in front of me. "*No.*" I've never been much for gossip but this is too juicy not to partake in. "You and Unnith?"

"So you're not a completely useless lesbian."

"Wow. I expect gay on gay violence at my apartment but here?" I shake my head, still trying to piece it all together. The gossip from earlier this summer, about Unnith and the bushes, hits me harder than a brain freeze. "Wait, was that *you?* In the bushes. Cocktail night?"

Carl shrugs. "Yeah."

I need a second to take it all in. Brain freeze racks my brain or maybe I'm just short-circuiting at the image of Carl and Unnith— nope, not thinking too hard about that. "Why?"

Carl just puts up two fingers. I frown. "He… eats you out? I guess a forked tongue would be–"

"Don't make me retract my earlier statement."

"Look, I'm working with a handicap. I don't know what guys are into."

Carl drops his hand and crosses his arms. "Fair." He leans across the counter and speaks in a whisper while I suck down fruit pulp. "He's got two."

"Sounds like extra work," I deadpan. "But if it floats your boat." One is enough for me and only when it's attached to a pretty girl.

"Whatever," Carl drones. "If anyone was going to catch me in this situation, it's good it's you. You're not coming back next summer, right?"

"Not if I can help it…" I don't have to work here to see Steph. Or I shouldn't have to. "Since I'm already your confidant–"

Carl scowls. "Don't push it."

"Hear me out, I just wanna know what was going on with cocktail night. Like, if you and Unnith had an arrangement, did other people?"

Carl purses his lips, his eye still a narrow slit focused on me like a laser. "It was a swingers thing. In theory."

"Can anyone be a swinger in theory but not in practice?" I set aside my drink resting my chin in my hand.

"Sure. In theory you and your spouse are cool with fucking other people. In *theory*, but in practice, a lot of people didn't like seeing the mother of their kids sucking off John from down the street."

I frown. "People really didn't think that thought?"

"Rich pricks think with their gold plated dicks. People get bored. The smart ones just buy a luxury car or some other useless toy. Everyone else does something reckless."

Carl makes it sound like only rich people would end up in a situation like this. There are plenty of kids at school *trying the poly thing* instead of breaking up. But that's not what Carl is saying. No one wanted to fuck their neighbor because they didn't care about their spouse. Maybe they didn't even really want to get sloppy with someone they'd run into at the grocery store. It was the thrill they were looking for. And Serpent's Oasis offered it with a drink on the side.

Something shiny and new, unique and sexy. The fruit in my stomach suddenly isn't settling so well.

"But yeah, that's why we don't do cocktail night anymore. Too many people got upset after getting exactly what they wanted. Customer service at its finest." He pushes off the counter and starts gathering things in the kitchen. "I'm gonna make a quesadilla. Want one?"

"Sure…" Despite the unease in my stomach I know better than to pass up free food.

The frying pan sizzles as Carl shows me two salsa options. I go with mild, just in case I really am going to be sick later. "Why do you still fuck around with Unnith?"

"I told you–"

"Oh cut the crap. You know what I mean. It's not like there aren't any other Dragonfolk around. Or dating apps. Hooking up with your boss sounds pretty reckless to me."

Carl is silent as he puts a large tortilla in the pan and spreads some cheese and salsa. "Convenience?" He offers with a shrug. "It's always been mindless sex so… I've never really thought about it to be honest."

It's a flimsy excuse but maybe that's all there is. Lord Unnith is a bit of a freak, Carl is into DP, neither of them sound interested in anything more. I guess they're kind of a match made in heaven. Or HR Hell.

"But you're right. It is pretty reckless. Guess I like that part of it too. But don't get it twisted. Unnith and his wife are proper swingers. She knows all about me. Probably more details than I'd like her to know."

"Your dick isn't gold plated but you're still thinking with it."

He points at me with his spatula. "Don't think I've forgotten about you and Mrs. Donis." He flips the quesadilla.

"What's going on with that anyway?" I must make a face because he adds. "I spilled the tea now you've gotta share. It's like you've never kikied in your life."

"I'm not one for gossip that involves me." Yet I roll my shoulders back and keep talking. "She likes to buy me things. I like eating her out. That's the arrangement."

Carl is quiet, nibbling at his bottom lip. "Unnith gives me shit if we're short fifty cents at the end of the night." He plates the quesadilla and cuts it up before setting it down between us. "Well, congrats, sounds like you're living the dream."

"Don't tell anyone okay?"

"Does anyone else know?"

I shake my head. We lock eyes, which is a little strange when Carl only has one, and make a silent agreement. As fun as it would be to see Jessie freak out, it's not worth putting Carl's job on the line. "Jessie was right," I grab a slice, "you're a pretty chill manager Carl."

"Because I made you food or because I fuck my boss?"

"Because you haven't shouted at me for closing the pool early." I shove food in my mouth and he snorts, shaking his head.

CHAPTER
Nine

CLOUDS FINALLY BREAK as I'm getting off work. I hide under the awning to avoid the raindrops. When I check my phone there's a text from Steph and one from Goldie. Steph's text is brief, just her letting me know she's on her way to pick me up. I open up Goldie's text.

> Have fun tonight! We know you're sleeping over at a friend's so just let us know when you're on your way home. Would be so awkward if you walked in on me dancing naked around the apartment or something lol

> Are you worried me seeing you naked would be awkward or worried Jessie would get jealous if I saw you feathers and all? I'll keep you posted. Sorry for scaring you the other night.

> Jess has seen me naked too many times to be jealous 😊 lol don't worry about it. I figured you were fine but Jess gets freaked out.

> I guess everyone needs a mother hen every now and again.

When I look up from my phone a familiar sports car sits in the rain. I cover my head with my bag and run. It's a pain getting down so low to slide into the cab. "Sorry about the seats." I tell Steph as I shut the door.

She laughs. "There's no point in using this car if the seats don't get a little wet." She winks at me.

We go slow in the rain, the engine practically silent when it's not pushing the throttle. I take in the views, the entire neighborhood made up of large houses with vibrant green yards. Some of them have fancy art pieces that would fit right in at MOMA. Others have gazebos poking out from the backyard or tall staircases just to get to the front door.

Steph pulls up to a beige house with dark green wood edges. It's large, sure, clearly three stories, but it hardly seems as massive as the other houses we've passed. The garage door opens and we escape the rain. "I guess this is your... Well you've been here before, but you've never really seen the place."

Steph leads me inside to what I first think is an unfinished basement, the wall facing us made up of large stones. She points to her left down a corridor. "Wine cellar is over there." She casually keeps walking like what she said isn't absolutely wild.

We pass through what looks like a daycare; lots of toy chests, a mini plastic slide, small trampoline, fairy lights– a kid's dream. "The playroom. I wasn't sure if the no-windows thing would be a problem but I figure when they're teenagers they'll be down here all the time anyway. Might as well start them young."

"If the wine cellar is right there, yeah I'm sure they'll love it as teens."

"Oh the cellar is locked, only mommy has the key." She heads upstairs. We haven't even explored the first floor and I'm already lightheaded.

Large windows fill up the entire walls facing out over the

lake. I've been expecting them. Even on such a dreary day the view is beautiful, sort of haunting with the lake surface rippling with raindrops. It reminds me of home, of afternoons looking out over the lake while sitting on the roof of my childhood home.

"You've seen the kitchen and dining room. The sunroom is over here."

I follow in silence. The room off on the side of the house is all windows and rich redwood. There are doors leading out onto the patio just like in the living room. For the first time since entering the house I catch Steph's gaze. She tilts her head.

"I'm still caught up on the wine cellar thing."

She bubbles with laughter. "Why?"

"I don't know. Maybe it just feels like something a serial killer would have."

"Well now that you know my secret…" There's an ominous pause before she cackles with laughter. I sigh, not realizing I was holding my breath till just then. Which is so silly. I never need to hold my breath for anything.

"Is that revenge for bringing you to that slasher movie?"

"Just a little." She takes my hand. "You seem tense."

I swallow, "I am…" I spread my fingers so there's more space for my digits to slide across hers. I touch her fingertips. She traces the edge of my webbing. "I've never been in a mansion before."

"You have."

"Never in the daylight."

Steph gives me a slow nod like she understands now. "I don't know if this helps but for this weekend, this is *your* mansion." There's a rush down my spine. "I want you to be comfortable. So sit wherever you like, drink whatever you want, dance naked through the halls."

I lift a brow. "Why do I sense an ulterior motive?"

"If I told you to put on a show for me, you would."

She's right.

"But that's not what I want. At least not right now." She takes my other hand, lifting them both and making a show of interlocking our fingers. "Right now I want you to take this all in and appreciate it. Who knows. Hopefully one day you'll have a house with twice the number of windows."

We hold hands as she leads me through the rest of the house, to her office, the at home gym, the dining room with a table that could fit into a banquet hall. We haven't even touched the second floor. "How long have you lived here?"

"It was a wedding present to myself." There's an open entryway from the dining room to the kitchen. Steph goes to the fridge and grabs herself a can of something. "Would you like anything? I've got some seltzer and kombucha. Oh and plenty of juice."

"Do you have the stuff to make green tea shots?"

Steph blinks, then looks back in the fridge. "I might be able to whip something up…"

Before us on the counter there's lemon-lime seltzer, whiskey, peach schnapps, and a bottle of lemonade. Steph pouts as she holds a shaker. "I don't have any sour mix…"

"Isn't the alcohol the most important part anyway?"

With that she adds everything to the shaker, measuring with her heart. "This will probably taste more like a lemon-drop than a green tea shot but oh well." She grabs some shot glasses from a cabinet. Pouring out the mixture it just looks like normal lemonade. Not a single drop spills over the edge of the shot glass.

"How'd you acquire this skill?"

"Everyone should know how to mix at least one cocktail. Makes for good conversation." She slides over my shot then raises her own. I follow her lead and we tilt our heads back together. The sour hits my tongue first, then the sweet. I can't taste the whiskey at all.

"It's also helpful when you get invited to your boss' house

for the holidays." She explains. "Not every corporate event is held at hotel bars and restaurants."

I nod. "Everyone loves the coworker who makes the drinks." I think about Carl and the quesadilla he made me.

"It's never made me any enemies." She starts to put away the ingredients. "But I don't want you drunk tonight. Let me make us something a little lighter."

I don't object and she gets right to work. It's fun watching her navigate the space she clearly knows by heart. Not a bad view either when she gets up on her toes to grab a glass from the top shelf.

There's still this tension in my body and it takes a moment to recognize where its' coming from. My gut, still uneasy after my conversation with Carl today. There's no casual way to say, *I heard about the swinger sex parties they use to hold at Oasis, you ever go?* Steph's never been shy when it comes to sex. A little flustered at first, but she'd never been with a woman before. I like when she's flustered anyhow.

Steph finishes the cocktail and we relocate to the sun room. The patter of rain fills the room. Steph and I sit and chat about our childhoods. She spent a lot of time with her grandparents down at the shore and has always loved the ocean. The little beach town is easy to compare to my home-town. It's far from a tourist spot but we'd get the occasional adventurer passing through.

"I haven't been back in a while," I admit.

Steph hums as she finishes a sip of her drink. "You should visit after you graduate."

The suggestion doesn't spark anything within me. Not even disgust. Maybe it's the alcohol or the ambiance but I'm finally starting to relax. It's easy to relax when those lines appear around Steph's eyes, a dozen little smiles while I tell her about my high school swim team.

Once we've finished our drinks our hands are free to reach for one another. It's innocent enough at first. My hand on her knee and her hand atop mine. Then she guides me up her thigh, lets me slip a finger in the waistband of her jeans. She moves closer to rest her cheek on my shoulder. "You smell like sunscreen," she smiles against my neck.

I stroke her hair. "Tell me about the videos you've been watching."

"I can show them to you."

"You will," I assure her. My hand pulls back from her jeans and I run a finger along the denim edge. A bit of her stomach spills over, lined with pink stretch marks, and I love its softness. "But I want to hear you talk about them first."

Steph hums. "It was hard to find good ones at first. A lot of them just weren't sexy. It was like watching someone flirt *way* too hard. Too porny. When I finally found a good one I searched up the actress and looked through her stuff."

I could tease her and say I've got competition, but I want to understand her desire better. "What did you like about her?"

"In the first video I saw with her she was with a guy but she was in charge. It was sort of lady dominatrix at first. She kept calling the guy a pervert for liking her tentacles while she gave him a handjob. Tentacle-job?" She looks at me for confirmation but once dicks are in the equation I'm just as lost as she is. "Anyway, she started out all mean but got nicer as it went on. Maybe that's what I liked. That and the tenta-cle-job.

"I ended up paying for her website. I haven't bought porn since the 90s and that was for a college party where we all got wasted and just laughed at how ridiculous it was. It was worth the money though. I think she films her own stuff so it's more... down to Earth?"

"Less porny?" I smile.

"It feels more like pleasure and less like a performance. Plus she had videos giving tips to people who want to experi-ence tentacle play. How to be safe if your partner has the appendage and what toys to buy if they don't. She has a couple videos where she used a tentacle toy on herself."

I touch the button at the front of her jeans. "You'll show me that one, won't you?" Before she can answer I undo it, sliding my hand down past her zipper and caressing her pussy.

"Oh I'll show you so many videos. But first–" She removes my hand and stands up. "Let me slip into something more comfortable."

I follow her upstairs. I should crawl behind her, show her my excitement, my devotion. But I move a lot faster on my legs and I'm already impatient.

In the master bedroom, Steph stands in the bathroom entryway. "I'll be right back." She shuts the door.

Without her in the room to distract me I take in the interior. There's more large windows, the entrance to a walk-in closet, and jewelry boxes on the vanity. On the bed I see a pink robe laid out. I approach it, notice its embroidered on the breast. *Guppy.*

I strip and put on the robe. The fabric is silky and cold against my skin. Pink isn't normally my color, but it reminds me of Steph's nails so I'm happy to wear it. Catching a glimpse of myself in the mirror, with the bright pink fabric and my blue tinted skin I look like cotton candy.

"Dear," Steph calls through the door. I step forward, expecting her to ask me for help. Instead she tells me, "Sit on the bed for me. Have you seen my gift?"

I smile. "Guppy?"

"Perfect! Wait just one more moment."

I sit on the edge of the bed, watching the door like a I've been awaiting her for years. It creaks open. Steph is wearing dark blue and black lace. It pairs perfectly with her black and silver hair. Her thick thighs are contained by a pair of fishnet stockings. I lick my lips not sure where to look. At the dark blue lace that dances along her chest or at her hips.

In an instant she's straddling my lap and I remember we have all night. That I've got all weekend to drink her in. Maybe I can finally memorize her body. There are things I'll never forget, the heft of her breasts and those pale stretch marks.

It's not enough. I want to count her stretch marks with a kiss on each one. Want to be able to recognize her just by touch. If there is a grey hair on her head I want to know about it.

Steph tilts her head as she looks down at me. "My laptop is in the bedside drawer."

"What else do you keep in those drawers?" I sound like I'm in a dream, my voice airy and a bit distant.

"Cheeky," Steph chides. She gets off my lap and goes for the bedside table. It feels like a punishment at first till I turn and get a perfect view of her ass. Something about the garters make her ass look even rounder. I think about smacking it, wanting to see her ass ripple like water, but she turns over and opens up the laptop. I shift to sit beside her.

Some videos are already loaded up. I see what Steph means by too porny just from the titles. "Big tit beauty gets POUNDED by tentacle dick." "My step-sister rides my tentacles." "Busty redhead impregnated by tentacles." The most creative by far is "TENTACLE GANGBANG"

Steph's face is bright red. She's been pretty cool and collected so far, but most people would be pretty embarrassed showing off their porn preferences. I touch the trackpad and press play on the big tit beauty video. Who doesn't like big tits?

From the very start the video is living up to its title. A woman with breasts even bigger than Steph's has some tentacles between her breasts, bouncing them up and down to caress the writhing appendages. It's a POV shot, only the lower half of the other performer in the frame. Fishfolk genitalia is the same regardless of gender or even subspecies.

Soon the woman is on her back with her legs spread wide. The tentacles waste no time, some slipping inside her while others caress her cunt or suction to her legs. She bucks her hips, chest bouncing. Her moans are loud, rich baritone that is over the top sure, but nice to hear.

I lean into Steph's ear. "Don't tell me you just *watch* these videos."

Steph purses her lips. "If you want to watch me touch myself dear, you should just say it."

"I want to watch you touch yourself." I kiss her earlobe. "Please."

Steph smiles to herself. Before she honors my request she switches to a different video. A Fishfolk woman with jet black hair and orange scales sits on her knees. When the video starts I know exactly what this is. The performer Steph says she likes with a large tentacle toy between her legs. It's pretty phallic, much larger than any of my tentacles.

The woman starts riding the toy, her own tentacles reaching for it, pulling her further and further down the base. Steph finally slides her hands down her curves. She spreads the lips of her pussy and I see the panties are split down the center. Her fingers dip past the fabric.

"Fuck," I breathe, just watching her. I don't have anything on to contain myself, my tentacles already coming to life, a slippery wetness dripping down my upper thighs.

Sound erupts from the laptop and the woman's thighs shake as pale white liquid cascades down the toy. Steph hums and I catch her slip a finger inside herself. The video continues to a different shot, the Fishfolk woman on her hands and knees with another woman behind her. The toy is now attached to the woman's crotch with familiar straps.

A voice coos from the video. "You want this? What to get fucked like a good little bitch?"

"Lydia," Steph whines. "It's no fun doing this alone."

My robe is open now my tentacles poking through like

they're waving to Steph. Maybe they are. I adore every part of her, every part of me adores her. I slip my hand between my thighs, push past my tentacles and rub myself slowly.

Steph hums with approval. "That's a good girl. Show mommy how you touch yourself."

I flutter my eyelashes. "Yes, mommy."

The videos keep going. It's always the same Fishfolk woman with scales that remind me of a goldfish, but she has plenty of friends. I only remember the highlights; her taking two toys at once, two women on their knees sucking on her tentacles, a round of frontage with another Fishfolk. Watching the two women's bodies shiver as their tentacles intertwine is more than enough to finish on my fingers.

Of course I watch Steph too. She fucks herself hard and fast, causing slick squelching sounds, but always pulls back right before she's about to finish. Leaving her sitting there, chest heaving and skin flush. Her panties are still on but soaked through.

The words slip past my lips without me thinking. "I want to taste you…"

I was hoping she would straddle my face but mommy knows best– she shoves her wet fingers in my mouth, tasting of sweet citrus. "There," Steph giggles. "Keep playing with yourself little Guppy." She slowly slides her fingers in and out of my mouth. I press two fingers inside myself, following her rhythm. "It's so cute how your tentacles react," she tells me. "How they wrap around your wrist… How they clean you up and make a mess on my bed."

Past her fingers I manage to say, "I'm sorry."

"No sweetie, don't be sorry. I want to see you all messy and spent." She pushes a strand of hair past my sweat soaked forehead.

Soon we forget about the laptop. Loud vulgar sounds still pour from its speakers, but we just look at each other. Laying on the bed across from each other as we touch ourselves.

Steph plays with her breasts in one hand and her clit with the other. I have one hand working my cunt, the other stroking my clit. My wrists aren't enough and I buck my hips.

My teeth capture my bottom lip, suppressing my little whimpers of pleasure. Steph's soft lips hang open, moaning and saying filthy things. "I want you inside me– I want you to fill me till I'm spilling. You look so pretty covered in your own cum. I want that. Please– please, Lydia."

Even with her words we never reach for each other. It would be so easy, but it's hotter if we don't. I've always wanted to know how she touches herself. Watch her back arch as she fills herself to the knuckle, see how flustered she gets when she edges herself.

When we do touch, it's to taste each other. Steph smears her finger across my lips. I pluck eggs from my tentacles and place them on Steph's eager tongue. She holds them there, letting me soak in the sight, before swallowing them. Then she opens her mouth for more.

My wrist starts to hurt. Steph's fingertips prune. We both struggle to go as hot and hard as we had previously. Finally Steph rolls over and rests against my chest, her hands nowhere near her pussy. I follow her lead, wrapping my arms around her, hugging her close. This tender moment is somewhat ruined by the porn still playing in the background.

"Oh yeah fuck my slutty hole with your tentacle cock!"

Steph snorts. Then she snickers, shaking her head. I laugh with her and we feed off each other, laughing and cackling together.

CHAPTER

Ten

BIRDS CHIP OUTSIDE, waking me. Steph is in my arms, the lingerie replaced with a soft nightgown. I'm still wearing the pink robe she bought me. I smack my lips, my mouth dryer than a desert. "Steph," I croak. I hope her sheets don't smell like fish after this.

She stirs, only to turn and bury her face in a pillow. I push the grey around her temples back behind her ear. "I need to take a bath." I sound like I have a cold, everything stuffy and dry.

Steph lifts her head and yawns. "Okay…"

She doesn't get right out of bed but eventually rolls onto her feet and heads for the bathroom. There's a fancy looking shower with several jets built into the wall in addition to a flat rain shower head on the ceiling. Steph rubs her eyes with the palm of her hands. "Is a shower okay… There's a bathtub in my kid's bathroom."

"Shower is good." Soaking would be better for my scales but I've never seen a shower this fancy. I want to try out all the different settings.

Figuring out the top shower head is easy enough but after that I get lost pretty quickly. Past her sleep Steph notices me struggling and pokes past the glass wall. "You have to turn that center nob. It'll go through all the settings like–" A loud yawn. "Like those garden hose attachments. It's annoying…"

I turn the nob and two flat beams of water mist my body.

"I'm gonna go make breakfast…" Steph says and shuffles off.

I sort of thought she'd be a go-getter morning person. What with the fancy job and two kids. I guess fancy late night dinners and cocktails she knows by heart that say otherwise… Is anyone both a morning person and a night owl? Seems like they would conflict schedule wise.

After spending a ridiculous amount of time fiddling with the different settings I settle on what I think is the highest setting. Jets of water spraying me on the side while gentle rainfall hits me from above. Baths will always be my favorite but this is like unlike anything I've experienced.

When I step out of the shower I pat myself dry and put my pink robe back on. As I descend the steps I can already smell eggs and coffee. Steph stands at the stove, holding a coffee mug in one hand and a skillet in the other. "Good morning!" The sleepy zombie is gone, replaced with bubbly hospitality like she's the owner of a renowned Bed and Breakfast.

"Wow. Have you seen Steph? Last I saw her she was half awake and grumpy like a feral cat."

"Grumpy!" Steph frowns. "I just hadn't had my coffee yet," she pouts. "There's more in the pot, do you take sugar? Cream?"

"I take it black," I offer her a soft smile. "And I'll take those eggs."

While Steph cooks I sip on some water and watch her. The rain has stopped but the sky is still a pale grey. "Anything you want to do today?"

"You mentioned that auction gala thing…"

Steph nods, not looking up from the skillet.

"I want a new suit for it. We could get that today."

Steph's smile is brighter than a sunny side up egg. "Perfect." She plates the egg, hands it to me, and kisses my cheek. "Let me go make a call."

She leaves me standing alone and confused in her kitchen. So I head to the sunroom to have breakfast, lounging across the couch. Fog hangs over the edges of the lake in eerie contrast to the birds singing triumphantly. The maple trees hide the other houses across the lake and I have to squint hard to notice their large windows. It's so easy to pretend like I'm somewhere far away from here. In the wilds of the Pacific Northwest or maybe even farther north up in Canada. Easy to forget there's a major metropolitan highway two miles away from where I'm sitting.

Steph joins me with her own plate of eggs and her mug of coffee, still wearing her nightgown. "I got us an appointment at Horn & Driver Custom. They do great work." She sits on the opposite edge of the couch, our legs touching.

"You're getting me a custom suit?"

"All good suits are custom. Remember? No suit arrives tailored to the right person. That's the artistry of a good tailor." She sips her coffee. "They could only get us in at three so we're in no rush."

"Do they sell cufflinks too?"

"Yes, but nothing custom." She smiles. "Do you want something custom?"

"Honestly? I don't know. I've never actually bought cufflinks."

"I know a good jeweler on 47th street. Well, who doesn't know a good jeweler on 47th street?"

"Me?" I offer. I know what she's talking about. Kind of hard to miss the storefronts that blind you with sparkling jewels protected by golems.

"You'll meet him, he's brilliant. But if we want to hit him

up we should get ready. Nothing is worse than traffic on a Saturday."

———

I THOUGHT Steph speeding down the highway was impressive but seeing her navigate through slow traffic is a whole different skill. One she's also mastered. She manages to slip into the fast lane, then slide right back out when it inevitably slows down. Truthfully I'm not sure it saved us any time but it makes the trip more interesting.

It's a humid day, the clouds above too pastel to threaten rain and the sidewalks still soaked from last night. The city is as busy as ever but Steph can swerve through people with the same ease as she swerves through traffic. Though I do have to ask, "Shouldn't we just take the subway?"

Steph sticks out her tongue. "In this heat? I'll melt down there."

We make it to 47th, the diamond district. I've passed by these shops plenty of times but never dared to step inside. With so much precious merchandise I expect them to check me at the door, demanding I flash a black credit card or a stack of hundred dollar bills. Of course nothing of the sort happens when we enter, but there is a tough looking Minotaur with a security shirt at the front entrance.

The shop reminds me of the beauty counters at the mall. There are dozens of glass cases, a number stuck on the edge of each one. I snag a paper map attached to one of the cases and realize there are at least twenty shops in this room. With so many cases the shop quickly turns into a labyrinth. Thankfully Steph knows exactly where she's going.

A short, stout man with tan skin and tusks jutting from his bottom jaw perks up when he notices Steph. "Stephanie! Good to see you, what a surprise, what brings you in?" As we get closer I realize he's wicked short, like standing on a step stool short.

She pushes her sunglasses to the top of her head. "Good to see you too Parth. I'm actually shopping for a friend."

"Hi," I wave, feeling out of place.

"Yes, come, I've just put out some new pieces today."

I do as he says and get right up the glass. Diamonds the size of my thumbnail sit on gold chains surrounded by even more diamonds in intricate patterns. One reminds me of a flower while the other is a more standard circle design. I glance at Steph, wondering what her reaction would be if I pointed to the necklace and told her *"That one."*

But I stick to the plan. "I'm looking for cufflinks."

Parth's nostrils flare and he makes a sound like a horse. "Ah, I don't have much, but…" He leans in. "I know the good shops in here," He points around at the other cases. "Not everything here is best quality. Stephanie and her friends always get the best quality. You know what gemstones you want?"

"Diamonds?" I suggest.

Parth lifts a brow. "I'll show you what to look for."

He takes some things out of his case and explains to me the basics, about a diamond's clarity, the different cuts, treated versus natural colored diamonds. I try to retain as much information as I can.

"Cufflinks will be a smaller carat of course, round cut typically, but I've seen some stunning baguette cuts. You have a map?" I hand him the paper and he circles a booth. "My friend Noah has a good set of cufflinks you should look at." Steph appears beside me, our shoulders touching. Parth lifts his head. "Are you sure nothing for you today, Stephanie? I just got a shipment in of some lab growns, we could create something custom for you."

"Not today. I've got so many beautiful pieces from you I

hardly ever wear as is. But we'll stop by to say goodbye before we leave, promise."

"Please! I'd love to see what you purchase."

We head to Noah's booth, Steph holding the map.

"Nothing in here has prices…" I notice.

"Oh no one shares the price till you're already wearing it, after you see just how stunning the piece is on and you're already in love with it."

"Convenient."

Thanks to Steph we find our way to Noah, a Human man with a well trimmed beard and thick head of curls. Inside the case he has cufflinks, some watches with diamond inlays, and thick banded rings. He pulls out the cufflinks display. "Feel free to pick them up, get a good look at them. Just set them to the side so I can polish them afterwards. And not on the glass, please."

I nod but the idea of holding something that costs half a semester's tuition so casually makes my palms sweat. Which can't be good for the gold plating or diamonds.

Steph takes the lead, grabbing a large cufflink with a thick diamond in the center. "This one would grab my attention."

"I don't want to be super flashy," I admit. "More classy. Old money."

Steph giggles, setting the cufflink aside.

I scan the different cufflinks but I keep being drawn to one set. Rectangle diamonds, a baguette cut, inlaid against a black and gold backing. As I pick one up, I hope Noah doesn't notice my hands shaking.

"Those are eighteen carat gold, so nice and sturdy. The black is rhodium, hand painted."

It's so simple but effective. The diamond is crisp and white like a diamond from a storybook. I hand it to Noah. "Hold onto these." I turn to Steph, "I want to look a little more."

"When you know you know."

I'm tempted by another set of cufflinks of a similar design but a different cut. Radiant I think? The rock is bulkier, the diamond larger. The first set I picked out still calls to me. Steph was absolutely right. "The baguette cut, that's what I want."

"All right," Noah nods. "I'll get you a box and we can ring you right up."

His back to us, I whisper in Steph's ear. "He still hasn't told us the price."

Steph waves her hand dismissively right as Noah returns with a box and old school calculator spitting out printer paper. "Cost breakdown is here," He rips the paper from the calculator, "The materials, labor cost, and tax."

"Naturally."

Steph is so casual despite the cost being over $25,000. We still have to buy a suit for those little things! I keep my cool, thinking back to Steph's smooth voice: *I want to spoil you.* Steph pulls out a checkbook and a few pen strokes later, I have my cufflinks in my hands. My heart races just looking at the box.

I'm in a daze as she leads us back to Parths's booth. He spots the box in my hand and grins ear to ear. "May I see?" He giddy like the box is for him. I open it up and set it on the counter. "*Very* sleek. Your friend has good taste Stephanie."

"That she does..." She slips her hands along my lower back. "Thank you so much Parth."

"Question– before you go." He tugs at his ears. "Earrings? Do you wear them?"

"Um... I work at a pool so not really. I do have them pierced."

He holds up his hand telling us to wait, then grabs a box that's not on the counter. "Simple, 24-carat."

The box opens, revealing a pair of small gold hoops. I pick one up, look in the mirror conveniently placed on the edge of the counter. They slide in no problem, hugging my earlobe.

Parth is right, they're pretty simple, but they're a brilliant color that rival Goldie's wings. I turn my head back and forth, admiring them.

When I finally stop staring at myself, Steph has her card in her hand. "You're a good man Parth, and a better businessman."

Parth laughs to himself as he punches numbers into the card reader. I peer over and am relieved when I see the earrings are only $2,000. At least we're sitting under 30 K in spending.

Outside, Steph pushes some hair back behind my ear. "They look even better in sunlight."

———

THREE O'CLOCK ROLLS AROUND and we step into Horn & Driver Custom. The place smells of leather and cologne, the walls lined with color coded suits. A young black man wearing a pinstripe suit greets us. "Welcome in, just want to let you know if you're here for a fitting we're all booked up today."

"We have a reservation," Steph tells him. "Three o'clock for Donis"

"Perfect. Right this way."

We pass the other store patrons riffle through the suits on their own. We're led to individual fitting rooms cut off from the rest of the shop. Our room is cut by a curtain, the open side with a mirror, couch, and a standing wine chiller with a bottle at the ready.

"Champaign is complementary. My name is Julian. I'm the only guy here with that name so just holler if you need anything, alright?"

I hadn't caught the accent in his voice till now. "Thanks, Julian."

"Your stylist will be here shortly."

Steph flops onto the couch. "Gosh all that walking has me tired…"

I walk up behind her, the couch between us as I wrap my arms around her neck. "Are you sure it's from walking and not from last night?"

"Maybe a bit of both."

The door opens and a person with green skin and large solid red eyes steps in the room. They have long spikes starting at their crown and descending down their neck. "Howdy," they smile, showing off sharp spindly teeth similar to the spikes on their back. "Names Mason, I'll be your stylist and tailor for the afternoon." They extend a hand and I take it. Mason has a firm grip and a leather bracelet with one of those cloth pin rounds attached. Instead of a cloth tie they wear a bolo with a turquoise charm.

I guess I should have expected this from a place called Horn & Driver. Though Texas isn't the first place I think of when I imagine good suits.

"Tell me 'bout what you're looking for today."

Steph is opening the bottle of wine and hasn't paid Mason much attention. I guess this is *my* suit at the end of the day.

"I'm looking for something professional– wait." I grab my cufflinks from Steph's bag and show them to Mason.

"Something to pair with these."

"When you say professional… What business are you in?"

"Nothing yet," I admit. "We're going to an event and I want to make a good impression."

Mason nods, stroking their chin. "Let me get your measurements." They wrap a measuring tape around my neck first, working down my shoulders and arms. Mason gets on their knees to measure my inseam. Steph watches the whole time, smirking.

"Do you normally do women's suits?" I ask.

"We do suits for all sorts. Designed my wife's suit for our wedding," Mason tells me with pride. "You sit tight,"

Mason says getting up off the floor, "We'll bring you some options."

I join Steph on the couch and she hands me a flight of champaign. "That's the second time today I've met someone and had no idea what species they are."

"Mason? Oh she's a chupacabra but I only know that from this article I read."

"About Mason?"

Steph nods as she finishes her sip of wine. "Last year they had a feature in the New Yorker about this place. Parth is, oh gosh I'm going to mispronounce this, Yaksha…" She says the name slowly, stressing the vowels. It sounds fine to my ear, so she's probably pronouncing it wrong. I'll have to look it up later.

We're halfway done with our drinks when Mason and Julian return with several suits. It feels like something out of a fairytale. There's red ones and blue ones, jet black and stoney grey suits.

I go for the bold suits first, curious how the red will match with my skin. It doesn't. "I like the cut…" I tell Mason though based on their expression they also don't think the color works.

It's nice to get input. Steph is happy to tell me what she does and doesn't like. Mason explains to me the different suit cuts, how the fabric typically behaves. Julian is in and out, making sure we're taken care of while also hyping me up.

Julian stands behind me. "I know it's been done a thousand times, but the black suit might be it."

I roll up the suit sleeve and examine the shirt button where the cufflinks would rest, imaging the gold and diamond in its place.

"It's been done a million-bazillion times," Mason agrees. "But you just might be right."

Julian turns to leave but I stop him. "You have ties and pocket squares, right?"

He smiles and I know a customer service face when I see one, but it still manages to feel genuine. "Course. You want me to bring you some samples?"

"I'm looking for a specific color." I reach for Steph's hand and show him her bright pink nails. "Can you get close to that?"

Julian leans in. Mason does the same. "Bold, bombastic pink. I got you."

Mason is still examining Steph's nails as Julian leaves. Her eyes shift to me, at least I think they do. Pupiless eyes always throw me off. "You want to stick to the black? That's an American cut right now, standard cotton and linen mix. Let me grab some mohair and silk suits."

Mason leaves and Steph and are alone for the first time in what feels like ages. "Are you sure you want pink?" She sets her wine glass down.

I slip my hands into my back pockets. "Why not? I can always change it. Plus black and pink are a killer combo."

"I suppose." Her finger twirls a streak of grey. "I just worry about us being obvious."

"I'll get a black tie as well," right as I say this Julian returns with a display of several pink ties. He and I take turns holding them up to Steph's fingernails. Her cheeks are starting to match her nails.

"Got it," Julian says. The cotton tie matches perfectly.

Like clockwork Mason returns with more suits. The first one feels perfect, not too heavy but the fabric holds shape around my shoulders making me look broader. I slip on the pink tie and do my best attempt at tying it. It doesn't look too bad but as soon as I step past the curtain Steph stands up and adjusts it. "You'll have to practice before the auction…"

I glance past her and Mason and Julian. "Uh… Mason could you go grab that one navy suit I tried on? And Julian, I'm also looking for a black tie. Or whatever. Just something basic that can go with anything."

The two leave while Steph is still fixing my tie. She runs her palm down my chest, smoothing out the fabric. I grab her wrists, spin her around so her back is pinned against my front. "Where's the fun in being subtle?" I whisper in her ear. I take her waist and sit down on the couch, bringing her with me.

In the mirror the image of her in my lap is breathtaking. Her brown eyes are wide with surprise. Her knees are together and back is straight like she's trying to get a good grade in class. I look crude in comparison, legs wide open to accommodate her. My lips still pressed to her ear.

"Oh," she breathes after taking it all in. "You look so handsome..." Her hand drags down my thigh. "I do like the tie with that suit."

"So that's a yes on the pink?" I watch her face through the mirror. Her surprise expression melts into a smile. She just nods then gives my knee a squeeze.

CHAPTER
Eleven

STEPH and I do a little more shopping, popping in and out of the other luxury stores that surround Horn & Driver. I get a new pair of aviators and don't take them off till we're at dinner. It's a cute little Italian place on the edge of Hells Kitchen.

"I want to take you somewhere," Steph tells me as we dine on calamari.

"I don't have a passport," I warn her. I'd love to drop everything and go to Europe with her. Any part of Europe. All of it is older and fancier than the US.

"Have you been to the shore?"

"Once. After finals freshman year. Bunch of friends and I took the train and made a day trip of it." I squeeze some more lemon over the fried squid before popping a cluster of tentacles in my mouth.

Steph makes a face. "Isn't that... a little strange for you?"

I shrug. "Plenty of Humans eat animal organs. I can't tell the difference between bull testicles and Human ones. Can you?"

She makes a face. "Fair enough. Anyway, back to the trip.

I could get us a hotel and we could spend a few days at the shore."

I hum, bouncing in my seat. "Can we go to Atlantic City?"

Steph grimaces. "Oh Guppy, you don't want to go to Atlantic City."

"Yeah I do," I laugh. "I'm pretty good at blackjack."

Steph smiles and rolls her eyes. "Dear, if you're dying to watch retirees play slots in cheesy hotels with questionable carpet stains we can absolutely go to Atlantic City. Or we can compromise and go to Brigantine Beach. It's close by."

"You know the shore better than I do."

"Asbury Park and Atlantic City are pretty far. Not even the same county."

"I mean I trust you to plan the trip." I touch her hand. "What matters is I'll get to see you in a swimsuit off the clock. Are there boardwalks in Asbury Park?"

"Absolutely. Gambling on carnival games is much more fun than slots I promise you."

The sun starts to set. The lights in the restaurant are kept low and everything appears illuminated by candlelight.

"When do you go back to school?"

"First of September."

July is almost over. I've been so looking forward to the gala event I'd completely forgotten that the summer is winding down. It won't be long till it's time to pack up my things and move back into the dorms. Replace afternoons by the pool with two hour lectures. Lifeguarding can be a drag but it's been nice sitting in the sunshine all summer. And meeting Steph of course.

"What about you? The kids I mean, when do they start school?"

Steph sighs. "Steven starts kindergarten on the first as well. I know it's not so different from daycare but he will be going to school with older kids. Fifth graders and stuff."

"What about Sophie?"

"She can go back to daycare whenever but I'm starting her a week earlier than Steven. She hates being separated from me or Roman. I just want her to be able to come home and have me there or pick her up if she's having a rough day."

"You're a good mom." I say as if I have any authority.

I don't know anything about marriage or kids, about owning a house or really just being a functioning adult. Steph is somehow able to keep it all together and handle me on the side.

"Is it boring?" I ask. Steph, understandably, lifts a brow. "The nine to five, and then the kids from five to nine."

"It's draining," she admits. "Especially when you don't have anyone to share it with. But at the same time it makes me feel more…" Her head teeters as she picks the right word. "Executive." The word lingers between us before she starts laughing. "That sounds lame doesn't it?" She picks up her wine, gesturing with the glass. "I'm an executive at work and an executive at home with my kids and my ex. It's not exactly what you want to read on a family Christmas card.

"But it's what I'm good at. Everything is a negotiation. Roman wants a surprise weekend with the kids? Well I better get Christmas and New Years this year. Steven wants to stay up late? Sure, if he helps me clean the kitchen counters. Sophie– well she's a little young to negotiate with, but she's getting better about sharing. Sometimes she lets me play with the pink mermaid if I ask nicely."

"She sounds like someone I know."

She hides her smile behind the edge of the wine glass. "I have no idea what you mean."

As she takes a sip, I realize something. "What about us? I tell you what I want and you give it to me. Except for Atlantic City."

Steph licks her lips. "I guess you're the exception. You're my outlet for submission."

I chuckle. "I don't really consider myself the dominant here."

She tilts her head. "Why not?"

I don't have an answer. It would be nice if I did, not just for Steph's sake, but my own. I wasn't the dominant one when I was with Ari, in the bedroom or otherwise. With Steph, I *could* be more bossy. Except I've never have to be– I ask, she gives and the few times she hasn't it's because she's able to give me something better.

"You just… know more than I do. You know about jewelry and nice suits. You understand business. You know more about yourself."

"You know me plenty well, dear." An ambulance drives by, the flashing lights making Steph's deep brown eyes appear red. "You knew before I did what I wanted– what I *needed*. I don't know if I'd even be able to gather up the courage and tell you… Tell you…"

She laughs awkwardly, "Gosh even now I don't know what to say. I understand what you mean, Lydia but we aren't exactly on an equal playing field. I'm twice your age. I've had so much more time to understand how everything works. There are qualities you possess that can't simply be learned."

I'm still baffled by her earlier question. Why don't I feel in control despite Steph offering that to me? It's what she wants and… It's what I want too.

"We're going to Atlantic City," I say firmly.

Steph's lips part, her eyes sparkling.

"I want to stay in a cheesy hotel with a big bathtub and drink surgery cocktails while we watch old people gamble away their retirement fund. Then we can waste all our money on carnival games and God knows what else." I rub my bottom lip, thinking up more demands. "You're going to wear a bikini every time we go swimming."

"Oh," Steph squeaks.

"Everyone is going to see just how fucking sexy you are."

I lean across the table, dropping my voice. "Then I'm going to take you back to the hotel room and fuck you like in all those videos you touch yourself too. You're going to be my personal hatchery. So full of me nothing will ever fill you like that ever again."

Everything moves around us but we seem frozen in place. Steph takes deep, slow breaths like she's trying to keep her heart rate down. I start to worry I've gone too far– but then she nods.

"Use your words," I say.

"Yes, Lydia. I will do all of that for you." Her foot slides up my leg. "I want you to use me. Change me. Make me *yours.*"

"Okay then," I sit back up and gesture for the waiter to come over. "We're ready to order." Steph blinks like she's just been snapped out of a trance. She fumbles for the menu, but I'm still talking. "She'll have the eggplant lasagna and I'll have the muscles in white sauce, please."

The waiter leaves and Steph stares at me, blinking away shock. "I... told you on the walk over they have a great eggplant lasagna."

"Couldn't help myself," I shrug.

Steph puts her elbows on the table, resting her chin in her hands. "No, please, continue. You can order us dessert next."

———

I TEXT Goldie and Jessie that I'd be home in thirty minutes after we cross the bridge back into New Jersey.

I stand on the sidewalk with my suit in a coat bag slung over my shoulder. The sun has set but I still wear my new aviators.

Steph leans across the front seat. "You sure you don't want help with that?"

My glasses slide down my nose, glancing over the metal

edge to look at Steph. "Sounds like you don't want to say goodbye."

"Am I that obvious?"

"A little. I love it." I give her a wink and head up to the apartment.

Inside, Jessie sits on the kitchen counter eating ice cream out of the tub. She practically drops her spoon when she sees me. "What... Did you get a new dress?"

"Suit," I correct.

Goldie slides open the balcony door. "Damn, look at you."

"She's wearing a tank top," Jessie drones.

"Yeah but she's strutting around like she's wearing a three piece suit."

I nod at the bag. "You want to see it?"

Goldie's eyes go wide. I set the suit down on the coffee table and unzip the bag. Goldie and Jessie surround it like surgeons at an operating table.

"Oh that looks good," Goldie grins. "I'm surprised you didn't get a flat top to match."

I chuckle, "Maybe someday but I like my hair long."

Jessie grimaces. "Not to be a downer but, are we going to be okay on rent this month?"

"I can send you my share now if you want."

Jessie and Goldie eye each other. "Okay, I'm gonna say it," Jessie announces. "This is weird."

"Jess," Goldie furrows her brows. "Lydia doesn't have to tell us everything about her life."

"What if she's in the mob?"

"She's a college student!"

"Kind of flattered you think I'm tough enough for organized crime." I zip up the suit. "But nope. Just came into some money and figured I should get a good suit."

Jessie looks skeptical. "And this has nothing to do with your friend you keep holding sleepovers with?"

"Hmmm," I consider my options; lying or giving her just a

crumb of information to nibble on. "It probably does."

Goldie holds up her talons. "But it's none of our business! Lydia pays rent, does her dishes, and hasn't flooded the bathroom."

"Oh so she's perfect?" Jessie snaps at Goldie, who looks hurt.

All things considered, I like Jessie and Goldie. It's nice of them to try and be my friends when they already have each other. It also looks to me like they've got some tension between them… Or maybe they just need to admit something to each other.

"Yeah so I'm gonna keep my suit in your room Jessie if that's–"

"That's fine, of course it's fine, it's always been fine."

"Right. Goodnight." I bail out of the living room, shoving my suit in Jess' bedroom closet before hiding in the bathroom. When I try to exit, Goldie stands in the doorway. She shuts the door behind us so it's just the two of us in Jessie's room.

"Sorry about her."

I cross my arms. "Do you always apologize for her?"

Goldie looks sheepish, her talons scraping together.

"Are we really the only two lesbians here? You are gay, right?" It comes off more accusatory than I intend, like I'm checking ID.

"I am." There's a pause. "I know there have been some awkwardness. I guess Jess wasn't ready for me to flirt so casually with you."

"I haven't taken it as flirting," I admit.

"Good. You're not really my type." She admits.

"Too scaly?" I offer with a smirk.

"Pretty much. I've only dated other Harpies. Less to explain, you know?"

I nod, "I guess the lesbian polycule is harder to explain to Humans. But it's not impossible, if you ever did want to date a Human. Or other monsters."

Goldie chuckles, her feathers fluffing up around her neck. "It's not like I grew up in a proper flock, just me, my moms, and sisters in a townhouse. Not exactly the cliffside nests you expect."

I shrug. "I grew up on land by a lake. I still consider the community I grew up around a pod." Even as I say it I know I didn't grow up in the typical Fishfolk manner. It's hard not to let Landfolk, Human expectations become the norm. My parents and grandparents are men and women, when in pods those genders don't really exist.

Some Fishfolk hunt while others protect the young and others still are in charge of singing and remembering the pod's stories. I'm not sure which one of those categories I would have floundered into had I been born and raised in the ocean.

As it stands I like being a woman just fine. Whatever that means.

"Jess had kind of a weird home life," Goldie starts.

I raise a hand. "I really don't need to know about all that. I'm not pissed at Jess, really."

Goldie frowns. "I'll talk to her. For my own sake."

I just walk past her and head for the bathroom. Before I run the bath I listen for shouting or a hushed argument. I don't hear anything. Which is for the best.

While the water runs I unpack my overnight bag, chuckling as I find the super pink, super short robe Steph gifted me. I grab a pink, cherry blossom scented bath bomb and drop it into the tub. I slip into the cool water, the perfect end to a humid day. My gills flutter, happy to be submerged. Once I'm relaxed I grab my phone and snap a couple pictures. Then I scroll, selecting one where my ass is framed by bubbles and sending it to Steph.

Miss you already.

CHAPTER

Twelve

Are you excited? :D

> Hard to tell what's excitement and what's
> nervousness. So yes.

Oh don't be nervous. Half the people are
going to be drunk anyway.

> I might join them.

> Everything booked for the Shore trip?

Yup! Hotel is booked and Roman is excited
to have the kids for a few extra days.

> Does that mean you get New Years and
> Christmas?

Yes, but it's already my year with them. Still
deciding when to cash in my extra kiddo
days.

> Do it on his birthday.

Oh that's mean. I'll have to remember that if
he keeps being grumpy.

This is going to be a good month.

It is! I'm glad I'm spending so much time with
you before school starts again.

Well we'll both be in the city, so we'll see
each other.

Dear I'll be working. You'll be working too!
And then I have to commute back home so I
can actually see my kids.

Right. How do you manage that?

Nanny does after school pickup and I try to
have one foot out the door at five. It's not
perfect. Far from it really but I'm making it
work.

You are. You make everything work, Steph.

You're making me blush. Save that suave talk
for the beach, Guppy ;)

———

I HAVE no idea what to do with my hair. All this preparation with the suit, the cufflinks, the tie– and I'm standing here with my mop of blonde hair wondering what to do. Goldie was right, I should have just cut it. Maybe it's not too late to go at it with a set of kitchen scissors. Totally not a catastrophic idea.

Nibbling at my bottom lip I find myself outside of Jessie' room. I knock. She responds through the door. "What's up?"

I open it just a crack. Jessie is sitting on her bed scrolling on her phone. "Do you… know how to do hair?"

She lifts a brow. "Sure? Open the door for real first." Releasing the knob the door swings on its hinges. Jessie sits up. "Brought out the suit?"

I've only got on the dress shirt and the suit pants, complete with the cufflinks and gold earrings. Not that you can see the earrings past my freshly washed, but still somehow unmanageable hair. "I'm going to a party with my friend who is totally not a mafia boss."

"Which is exactly what you would say if they *were* a mafia boss." She gets out of bed and joins me in the doorway. "Just do a braid or something."

"That's so basic."

"Okay, braid it on the side and throw it in a ponytail like you always do. Seriously don't stress, you're already wearing a suit and I assume a tie."

I rub the back of my neck. "Yeah, I guess you're right."

Back in the bathroom and start to wrestle with my hair. I've done a braid before. That's what I keep telling myself as I struggle to section my hair evenly and keep the braid flat against the side of my head. After two attempts I check the time– Steph should be here in half an hour and I still don't have my tie on. I gather all my hair ready to just throw it in a ponytail like any other day when Jessie and Goldie walk in.

"God you're a mess, let us help." Jessie grabs her wide tooth comb and brushes my hair out.

"You don't–"

"Yes," Goldie nods. "Yes we do." She smiles at me as she sections my hair, the tips of her talons feel good against my scalp.

With the two of them working all I do is blink and suddenly my hair is done. The braids are flat, pulling evenly from each section of my head on both sides like it was done by the same person. Jess sprays something into my ponytail and fluffs it up, giving it a little extra volume.

"Do you two have telepathy or something?"

"We used to do this on the playground all the time," Goldie explains. "It's been a while though. Gotta admit, I'm impressed with ourselves." They exchange a high five before interlocking their fingers and shaking their hand back and forth with a giggle. Either they worked things out or are just ignoring the issue. That or maybe there's always been a tension between them they've just accepted.

I'm too focused trying to get my tie perfect to investigate further. As I slip on the suit coat and examine myself in the mirror I recall all the things Mason told me makes for a good suit. The coat ends just above the wrist letting me flash my diamond cufflinks. There are clear creases in the pant-leg. When I sit, I make sure to undo the bottom coat button and check the pant-leg, seeing it rise just enough to flash my socks. Also pink, matching the tie and pocket square perfectly.

I wonder if I can send Julian a thank you card.

My phone buzzes and I don't bother to check who it is. As I leave I call over my shoulder to Goldie and Jess. "Thanks you two!"

Downstairs, Steph stands near her car and I have to catch my breath. She's dressed in a black dress to match my suit. Her shoulders are bare, fabric wrapped tight around her chest with sleeves down to her wrists. The skirt is much looser, more flowing. I mistake the black band around her neck for a necklace till she gets closer and I see it connects to the dress in the back.

"I couldn't wait till the auction to appreciate your outfit." She tells me.

"I'm glad you're impatient. You look amazing."

She pushes some hair behind her ear. Her nails are always near-perfect but I can tell she got them redone for tonight. Bright pink as always.

I take her arm and lead her the five feet to the driver's seat, opening the car door. "My own Princess Charming," she giggles.

Everything is so familiar now; the hum of the engine as Steph accelerates down the highway, the brief view of Jersey

City before we enter the tunnel, the looks from passersby who know all too well how much this car costs. I try to take it all in but it's hard not to think about how this might be the last time we visit the city. For a while. Till next summer, maybe.

We park the car a few blocks from the venue and I can tell we're getting closer when I spot the suits. Not the light grey and navy suits everyone wears in the city, but the jewel tone velvet suits, the tuxes and even some with boyish shorts. I guess when you always dress to the nines for a nine to five you've got to find new ways to mix things up. The outfits scream, *This is my fun suit!*

All the glamor clashes with the dozens of buses coming and going from Port Authority. Tourist are inescapable on Manhattan, especially during the summer, double it when you're this close to Times Square.

"You alright?" I nudge Steph. "You hate it here."

"Just so long as we don't go past 40th Street I think I'll live."

"What did Bryant Park ever do to you?" I ask.

"Oh hush."

Gotham Hall is lit up with purple lights in-between its marble pillars. When I first saw the building years ago I assumed it was a government building. Which it probably was at some point. Nowadays it's a venue hall for gala events and penthouse kid's birthday parties. I've always been curious about what it looks like inside. There's a line out the door like any club on a Friday night, just older clientele. Steph and I get at the back of the line, grateful to see people shuffling along.

"If your job is hosting this, you must know everybody coming."

"Not everyone here works for the company. There are shareholders, some movers and shakers– The standard old money families that get invited to all these events to boost the auction."

I notice a banner mentioning some children's hospital but I'm not all that interested in the auction even with Steph's money. Tonight is about connections. Everything hits me then, just how monumental this all is and I squeeze Steph's hand.

"Your tie looks good. Forgot to mention."

"I practiced," I breathe.

"It paid off."

We make it inside, the hall everything and nothing like what I expected. The room is a large circle with a dome ceiling that reminds me of the Capitol building. The walls are a white marble while the floor is different shades of wood with an intricate inlaid design. Which is to be expected. What I didn't expect is all the lights, the dome covered with shifting purple flowers and butterflies. There are tables in the center of the room but right now everyone is milling about. It really is like a club for people with pensions.

"Do you want a drink first or should I introduce you to some people?"

My mouth is dry. "Drink," I croak.

Steph somehow knows exactly where the open bar is. I get a water, she gets the speciality cocktail the same blue and purple as the lights above with a little fake butterfly garnish. Steph and I eye each other's drinks.

"What's with the butterflies?"

"Summertime? Hope? I'll have to pick our event manager's brain later." She shrugs and plucks the butterfly from the edge of the glass, shakes it off, then puts it behind her ear.

A man comes up behind Steph, touching her shoulder lightly. The second she catches him in her periphery she opens her arms for a hug, which he accepts. "Good to see you Stephanie, you never come to these things."

"I've had toddlers the past six years, Bobby. Haven't had the time."

Bobby is clean shaven and considering the wrinkles

around his eyes I'd say he's around Steph's age. There's plenty of silver in his short cropped hair. He's one of the guys wearing shorts down to the knee like he's about to go play disk golf, but the vest and suit coat keep things professional.

"Bobby, I want you to meet Lydia."

Without a second thought Bobby offers me his hand.

"She's a business student at NYU." Steph explains as I shake Bobby's hand. Though it's hard not to watch her as she talks, I'm curious what she'll say about me. "She's from the Midwest too."

"Whereabouts?"

"Michigan, around Presque Island but not actually Presques Island."

Bobby nods. "I'm from Wisconsin. Near Green Bay but not actually Green Bay." He laughs louder than he needs to, which makes me chuckle with him.

I feel like a fisherman pitching a lure. "How do you know Stephanie?"

Within the hour I've met a dozen Bobbys. Corporate suits all from somewhere other than New York eager to chat with little old me. I keep things professional, try to bring up school, the clubs I'm in, my favorite classes and what I hope to do in the next four years. Others are much less keen to talk about work, casually mentioning timeshares or their kids.

You have to relax a little if you ever want to land a catch. Especially a big one.

Steph and I end up back at the bar, alone for the first time in an hour. "You're doing great, I feel like everyone forgets I'm there the second you start talking."

"And I find it hard to not just look at you when everyone starts talking about their vacation to Aruba."

"That's business, dear. Even more than spreadsheets and dividends." She eyes the drink menu, pursing her lips as she reads.

I lick my lips. We haven't kissed tonight. Now isn't the

time but now that it's in my head it's going to be even harder to schmooze. I try to get myself back on track. "Who haven't I met yet that I absolutely should?"

"Have you met Alicia? She's the HR manager and the one who hires all the interns."

"Do you really think it's the best idea? Us working for the same company? In the same building? We wouldn't keep our hands off each other…"

"A quickie in-between meetings might up productivity," she argues. "I think Patrick Greysea is here."

I stand up straight. "The CFO of Triton Industrial? Here?"

"I didn't expect you to be such a fangirl. I don't know him personally, but pretty sure he and our CEO are buddies." Somehow she looks back at the cocktail menu like it's no big deal.

"Fuck that would be a killer connection. Not that he's going to be looking at resumes but–"

"You don't have to explain it to me. Come on." She hands me a glass of wine. "Let's go fishing."

Patrick Greysea has been in enough articles and magazine covers. I know what he looks like but there's at least two hundred people here. How many of those hundreds are just like me, hoping to make some connection tonight to help them get a leg up? Then I spot him, sitting at a table with another man.

I nudge Steph. "Is that your CEO?" Steph is looking in the other direction. I grab her shoulder. "Steph?" She jumps, eyes wide. I nod in the direction of Greysea. His suit is nothing flashy, deep blue pinstripes the same shade as his scales. His skin is a bit grayer than mine. A pair of black brow-line glasses rest on his nose. Even from afar he gives off an air of calm indifference. Or maybe that's just me being a fangirl like Steph says.

"You know who he's talking to?" I ask her again.

"Oh, um…" Steph shakes her head. "Shoot, I'm not sure."

I bite my lip. "We can't just go over–"

Steph takes my wrist and drags me over. "Oh my gosh," she practically shouts. Both men turn to the both of us. "Kevin is that you? It's been ages."

The other man, a Human with jowls and thick glasses, looks perplexed. "So sorry, I think you have me mistaken for someone else."

I take a big gulp of wine, my first proper drink of the night.

"Oh, no *I'm* sorry you just look like a friend of mine from college. I didn't mean to disturb you two. Stephanie Donis, I'm with Antswoft in marketing analysis." Steph shakes not-Kevin's hand first, then Mr. Greyseas like he's any other rando.

When Greysea lets go of Steph's hand, he looks at me, noticing me for the first time. I haven't spotted any other Fishfolk here. It might just be the two of us. I offer my hand. "Lydia Halloran."

Greysea shakes my hand. "Patrick Greysea. Are you also with Antsoft?"

"Not yet. I'm a student, NYU Stern School of Business."

"So then you know who I am," he says cooly.

"Of course. Even if I didn't, everyone who hears my major asks me if I'm going to be the next Greysea. Except you went to University of Chicago, right?"

"I did." He shifts his body, knees facing his buddy.

Fuck, I'm already losing him. "I played in the fountain there named after you." Greysea raises a brow. "When I was a kid." Hopefully he's not doing some quick math in his brain. Greysea does have a fountain named after him on the campus but they installed it when I was in high school. Even if the fountain had been named after him when I visited the campus as a kid, I was seven, I wouldn't have known who Greysea was or even cared.

He regards me with a nod. "You know, I wanted them to name a library after me."

"And you got a fountain? They could have at least named the aquatic center after you, bunch of smartasses."

He leans back in his chair. "Surely someone on the board is still having a laugh about it. Are you from Chicago?"

It's all pretty standard from then on. I tell him where I'm from, what I'm interested in, and yes, I do fangirl a little bit. Let him know I wrote a paper on Triton's business policy freshman year. I don't tell him I've been rejected from their internship program, especially not when he asks me if I've heard of it.

"I haven't," I lie. "I'll be sure to apply next time there's an opening."

He reaches into his breast pocket and hands me a card. I could scream, but I keep my cool, taking the card and feeling just a twinge of disappointment when it isn't his own. Instead it's for someone named Everett who runs the internship program.

"Email him your resume," Greysea tells me. "We run a tough program. Lots of dropouts. A resume and cover letter should be enough." He taps the back of the card. "His email isn't public."

I nod and slip the card into my breast pocket. "Thank you, Mr. Greysea. Have a good night."

I turn to grab Steph but she isn't here. It takes a few seconds of frantic looking to find her back at the bar. I'm so elated— talking to Steph isn't enough. I need to touch her, hold her hips while I babble on about how perfect tonight is. She's silent as I take her hand and lead her to the restroom. I lean against the bathroom counter and pull her into my arms.

"I know I'm getting ahead of myself but I spoke to fucking Patrick Greysea. For like, twenty minutes! Me!"

Steph's face is blank. My heart sinks and I wonder if I said something to Patrick I shouldn't have. Broke some unspoken rule you only learn about once it's already too late. Or maybe she's upset that I didn't notice her leave. "Steph?" I touch her cheek. "This is good right?"

Her eyes start to water. "Of course, dear." She shakes her head, voice cracking. "Sorry, my mind is somewhere else right now."

My heart falls to my stomach, bouncing and bobbing like it's ferrying a boat across choppy waters. Maybe it's none of my business. I should just try to distract Steph with a kiss and get her back out there with all the drinking and chatter. The auction is starting soon.

"You can tell me," I assure her. "Or... not. If you don't want to."

She laughs before blotting the corner of her eyes with her fingertips.

I'm not sure what sugar babies are meant to do when the sugar is on the verge of sobbing in front of them. I might overstep, might ruin this whole evening. But ignoring her tears and moving on doesn't feel any better.

"What's wrong?" I lift her chin. "Tell me. Please, Steph."

The first tear finally falls. "There's just someone here." She dashes away the teardrop with her palm. "I'm not even sure it's her but she just looked so similar... And the party is..." She shakes her head.

"Let's go for a walk," I decide.

We leave the venue hall and start walking south. Two blocks in I spot a bit of green space, one of those corners of respite that are all around the city. There's a statue of a woman with a shield and spear while two figures, a Human and a dog-headed person, hammering away at a bell. We settle in at one of the dozens of tables and chairs cramped into the small space.

"Fresh air helping?"

Steph shrugs. "A little... I'm sorry Lydia, I should have been able to keep it together–"

"You still haven't told me what upset you." I point out. Steph looks down at her lap. I place my hand on the table, palm up. I say it again, "Tell me."

She sniffles. "There was someone who looked a lot like one of our neighbors. I should say, she lived in the neighborhood. I don't know all that much about her."

I furrow my brows. The woman sounds like a stranger, so why does her doppelgänger have Steph so upset?

"Roman..." She hisses like someone is pulling out a deep splinter. "Slept with her at this party."

"Oasis cocktail nights," I say without thinking.

Her head shoots up. "You knew?" Steph's words drip with pain.

"All I know is that people were hooking up, swinging, whatever– but I didn't know... I didn't know *for sure* that Roman was involved." I'd assumed as much. It was easy to look at the guy and call him a cheater. Now in front of Steph things were a lot harder. More real and raw.

She starts crying silent tears dripping down her cheeks. "I'd had a couple drinks– but so had he, everyone was drinking. I wasn't drunk but... I told him he could."

"That doesn't mean he should have," I say. "Just because you said sure, he should have thought about it! About you."

"Lydia, everyone knew what those parties were about." She shakes her head. "I thought it... might be fun. We *both* agreed to it."

Cursing Roman out right now probably won't help Steph. Even if that's all I want to do right now.

I let her talk. "They hooked up and well... afterwards it just *ate* at me. I thought I was confident in us, in myself. That I wouldn't get jealous but I did. And whenever I talked to Roman about it, *tried* to talk to him about it, he said it was my idea. Said it wasn't fair to him that I regret it once it was too late..."

She blames herself. Or maybe the situation is just so

complicated she doesn't know who to blame. There's no perfect villain in this story, not Roman, not Steph, not even the other woman. It's a mess where you can't tell where one spill begins and the other ends. The kind of mess you hire a therapist for and I'm definitely not that.

I reach for Steph's hand. "It must have been overwhelming when you saw her tonight."

"If that was even her."

"But it wasn't *just* her, you said it yourself this is a big party where people get drunk and act a little reckless. So, just like the cocktail nights. Anyone would feel overwhelmed, Steph."

More tears fall, this time Steph wipes them away before they can slide down her cheeks. Smudging her makeup in the process. "God I'm such a baby."

"So? You're allowed to cry. And scream." I get up out of my chair, standing behind her to massage her shoulders. "Remember what you told last time we were here? That I'm your outlet?"

"But–"

I tilt her chin all the way back, forcing her to look up at me. Her tears fall sideways down her temples. "If anyone should see you like this... You're mine, Steph." Her brown eyes are so warm beneath the streetlights. "Let me have all of you. Even this part."

Her throat bobs, swallowing back another round of tears. "I feel so silly."

"Like I'd want to be with someone super serious." My lips curl in a soft smile. "Should we head home?"

To my surprise Steph shakes her head. "Let's go back."

"Steph–"

"I want to go back," she insists. I'm still holding her chin. "This night is about you. I wouldn't have bothered or even thought about it twice without you. Please, Guppy."

I'm not going to fight her. Steph using my little pet name

tells me she's going to be alright. She's strong like that, professional in every situation.

Steph gets up and straightens her dress.

"You'll want to freshen up in the bathroom before entering the ballroom," I warn her. "I'd help but I'd probably just smear your makeup more."

"Is that a promise?" She sniffles. "An invitation? It's been a while since we've fucked in public."

"As pretty as you'd look with your mascara running, I don't want to mess up my suit." I kiss the top of her head, just to assure her I do care more about her than some fancy suit. Black eye makeup has settled into the wrinkles around her eyes. Her skin looks less supple, tear tracks ruining her foundation. She looks so much older.

I can't help but kiss her again, finally on the lips.

CHAPTER
Thirteen

AUGUST ALWAYS GOES by too fast. Ever since I was a kid that coveted last month of summer has always felt too short. It's only worse now that I'm an adult dreading my full course load in the fall. Something tells me my 300 level classes won't start with a fun ice breaker and a casual stroll down the syllabus.

I'm getting ahead of myself. Maybe that's why this month always feels so short, my future responsibilities always overtake it.

Right now I need to stay in the moment. Even if that moment is traffic on the Garden State Parkway. Steph taps the steering wheel of her SUV. I grab my phone and start poking around Google maps. Atlantic City's reputation precedes it and I'd be lying if I said I knew anything about it beyond casinos and beaches.

"There's a lighthouse?" I think aloud.

Steph takes her eyes off the road, not that we're moving. "Of course. It's a beach town."

"Why is it so far inland?" There's at least three city blocks between the lighthouse and the beach.

Steph shrugs. "We could go visit and you can find out."

We haven't made many plans except spending as much time together as possible. That and making a mess of the hotel sheets. So a full itinerary, really. I am curious about the casinos but the beach calls to me. I swear I can taste the sea air just as we get onto the Atlantic City Expressway.

As soon as we pull into the hotel parking lot everything is taken care of for us. The valet takes the car, men in vests take our bags, and Steph just has to flash her credit card to get our room keys. I'm left standing there trying not to gawk at the lobby. Everything is so polished and shiny, nearly every table decorated with fresh flowers. People bustle past the balcony that overlooks the beach.

"Can we go to the beach first?" I blurt out in the elevator, sounding like a jittery kid who's been waiting all summer for this.

"Yes, dear. This is your vacation, remember?"

"Our vacation," I correct her. "I know you want to spoil me but it's more fun when we both decide what we should do. Besides, you know what's good down here. If I'd booked the hotel we'd be at Cesar's Palace."

"Oh… why there?"

I shrug. "I don't know what other hotels there are down here."

"You don't have to be staying at the hotel to use their amenities. If you can call the hotel lobby an amenity."

"The lobby here is super nice," I say just as the elevator door opens. "The views at every hotel I've ever stayed at have been parking lots and freeways."

The view from the lobby gave me a taste of our room view, but as always a little taste hardly prepares me for the full course. Our room is toned down from the lobby, the walls a welcoming beige instead of bright gold. Except the view is even better, a small balcony overlooking the ocean. I'm out there in a heartbeat, wind whipping through my hair as I'm greeted by the endless ocean. We're so high up I can see the slight curve of the island.

Funny that my first island vacation is in southern New Jersey but I'll take it.

Back in the room Steph is already undressing and putting on her swimsuit. I follow her lead, rummaging around my bag to find the brand new swimsuit I bought for the occasion. With Steph's money of course.

"A white swimsuit?" Steph giggles. "You're brave."

"I thought it would be cute if we were opposites." It was a bit of a risk but I've only ever seen Steph wear black bathing suits. Today she has on the black, stringy suit she wore the first time we hooked up. The string straining to uphold her heavy chest still makes my mouth water.

My suit is technically a one piece, with large half circle cut-outs on the sides exposing my gills. A silver ring holds the top and bottom of the suit together right at my sternum. As soon as I'm dressed Steph wraps a finger around the ring and gives it a tug.

"Easy," I warn her. "I know you're eager but let's get a little sunshine first."

Steph pouts. "But you look so good with this on... it just makes me want to see you without it."

"You can be patient," I say. "I'm not sure I can trust you to put on my sunscreen."

"Please?" Steph pouts.

I grab the tube of sunscreen and hand it to her before turning around, lifting up my hair to expose my shoulders. The swimsuit is backless, Steph touches me all over to make sure I'm covered. Her hands slide from back to my front, slathering my belly and hips as well. She kisses my shoulder to tell me she's all finished. Then it's my turn to do her.

She's showing off a lot more skin, though she has plenty more to show off. I take my time rubbing her back and neck, get down on the floor to do her thighs and calves as well.

"Lydia…" Steph whines. "You're making this so much harder for me."

"Good," I say in a sugar sweet voice. I hop up and kiss the tip of her nose. "The ocean will cool you off."

We grab towels and head down to the beach. It's crowded but easy to find space for just the two of us. Not that I linger on the sand for long. Ocean waves lap at my toes, the water cool but refreshing in the hot sun. Steph sits on the beach, watching me through her sunglasses.

Might as well give her a show. I wade into the water till it's up to my waist then dive into an oncoming wave. Pushing my arms down I propel further into the water, rocking my hips with my legs forming one fluid shape. I may not have a tail but it feels more natural to swim this way. Faster too.

The water is a crisp aquamarine and it's easy to spot the kicking feet of the other beachgoers. Little schools of silver fish dart around avoiding the landfolk. When I surface I immediately look for Steph. She's right where I left her, watching me with a smile on her face. I wave, kicking my feet to tread water. "Come on!"

To my delight she sets her sunglasses to the side and walks up to the water's edge. A wave rushes forward, soaking her ankles, but she doesn't walk any farther. A wave catches me and I let it propel me forward, diving just before it breaks and beaching myself right in front of Steph.

"How are the waves?" She asks.

I roll onto my back, looking out over the ocean. "They're nice." A large wave breaks ahead and I'm flooded with sea foam, Steph's calves now soaked.. My gills flutter with delight. "Are you going in?"

Steph scrunches her nose. "I'm worried about the waves taking my swimsuit."

"Don't worry." I reach back and grab her ankle. "Only I'm allowed to take off your swimsuit."

We giggle at my lame joke. I stand up and take her hand,

walking deeper into the ocean together. Once the water is up to our chests I lean back and float. The hot sun on my stomach and cool water lapping at my ears is a perfect combination. "I could just live here…"

"Why don't you? You can do that, can't you?"

"Most Fishfolk who live solely in the water are eccentrics. Off the grid types." At least that's what my parents told me growing up. I've never really looked into it much myself.

Steph floats nearby as she holds onto my shoulders. "But it wasn't always like that, right? I'll admit I don't know much about Fishfolk but I know about Atlantis."

"Atlantis sank," I point out. "It was a Human settlement first. Fishfolk are nomadic. We don't really build cities or have set homes. There are ocean pods still, but I'm spoiled. I like hot water and not having to hunt for my meals."

I don't notice the wave coming till we're already in its orbit. The crest crashes over both of us and we spin like we've been tossed in the wash. I surface no problem. The salt in my nose and mouth doesn't phase me. Steph pops up after me with a weak cough. Her head floats in the water, though the wave has pushed us to a more shallow part and I can stand no problem.

"Alright?" I ask.

Steph frowns at me. The water is clear and bright enough I can see her arms are crossed over her chest. Her neck is bare, no black string tied tight around her neck. "Oh shit–" I scan the water. "Stay right there!"

"Wasn't planning on moving…"

There's nothing floating nearby so I dive and linger in the water, feeling for the current. I let the water pull me, hoping it will lead me to Steph's missing swim top. I'm sure this happens all the time and Steph won't get in trouble for flashing the whole shore. I however, will be seeing plenty of pouts and frowns for the rest of the day if I can't find it.

I swim around, finding hermit crabs and seaweed but so

far no swim top. When I pop up to the surface to get a sense of where I am, I realize I'm way too far out. The beach life-guard stands up from his chair. I start swimming, a strong breaststroke so the guard can see I'm not in any danger. At least not from the ocean.

Steph has waded deeper in the water, probably sick of sitting in the sand. "Nothing yet," I inform her. Her frown is so severe it reminds me of a grouper. "I'm sorry, you were right–"

"What was that?" Her lip twitches as she tries her best to keep her scowl intact. "Sorry there's water in my ear. Say that again?"

"You were right," I tell her.

Her expression breaks as she laughs to herself. "Maybe you can make me a shell bra?"

"I still haven't given up." I dive back down, wondering if maybe the top is on the shore. Just then I spot something floating near the sandy bottom, mistaking it for seaweed at first. Steph's top is caught in a grouping of rocks nearby.

I swim over, hearing waves crash above me as I grab the fabric. The ties are all tangled in actual seaweed growing from the rocks. Being able to breathe underwater has never been inconvenient– but I'd be unable to free Steph's top without it.

Holding the top close to my chest I swim along the bottom, snaking around the dangling feet of swimmers up above. I stop in front of a familiar pair of thighs and surface. Steph blinks. I hand her the bikini top. "There might be some seaweed stuck to it," I warn her.

"Seaweed is good for the skin. Help me put it back on?" I tie the strings behind Steph's neck as she holds her chest. Once the little triangles of fabric cover her chest I tie in the back, making sure to double knot it. "Can I stick with a one piece for the rest of the trip?" she asks.

"I think you look great in both."

She turns around, wrapping her arms around my neck.

"Let's take a walk on the beach," I say.

We walk along the wet sand, hand in hand, sea spray keeping us cool. Most people just go about their day but some people shoot us glares. I expected that. What I didn't expect was so much anger from other women who appear around Steph's age.

Steph's stretch marks are visible, her stomach pokes out over her bottoms, and she has cellulite. Of course that also means she has thick thighs, a soft body, heavy and beautiful breasts. She's always been perfect to me. I don't expect other people to see it the way I do, but to be angry over it is so depressing.

One woman turns her head, following us as we walk past. I squeeze Steph's hand before whispering in her ear. "If I become old and bitter, mount me like a prized bass."

Steph covers her mouth to hide her giggles. I notice the woman scoff out of the corner of my eye.

———

I DON'T REALIZE I have sand in places it really shouldn't be till we're back inside the hotel. One perk of pools I completely overlooked this summer is the lack of sand. I'll take being slathered in lake mud over sand any day. "I need a shower," I sigh as we step into the elevator. "And a bath for good measure."

"I made sure this hotel room has both. We can freshen up before dinner."

The hotel shower is big enough that Steph and I don't have to take turns. We abandon our swimsuits on the floor and hop right in. I lather my hands with soap. Steph stands under the shower head and hums as steam fills the room. I reach out and start rubbing her shoulders but my hands wander to her chest.

"Guppy..." Steph whimpers as rub suds all over her

breasts. The soap creates a rainbow sheen across her skin and I find myself licking my lips. "You looked so beautiful today," She tells me. "It's terrible, but whenever I saw someone checking you out my heart raced."

I smirk as my hands cup her breasts, lifting and pushing them together. "Maybe..." My thumbs encircle her nipples. "Room service?" I give her nipples a soft pinch. "We'll both need the energy tonight."

Steph nods vigorously.

"Good girl," I tell her, then pinch her nipples harder. She gasps and leaves her plush lips open. Still playing with her tits I start kissing her neck. "Lucky me," I drag my teeth down her neck and then bite down on her shoulder. I whisper into her skin, "I have mommy all to myself." I kiss the already red and raised skin.

Steph slips her thigh between my legs and my tentacles latch onto her. I should show more control but I grind against her leg, the friction making my head spin. My fingers tease and tug at her breasts. More and more steam fills the room, Steph's whole body growing pinker by the second.

"Y-you can be rough with me," she tells me.

"I know." I lower my head and take her nipple between my teeth, carefully applying more pressure.

"Fuck," Steph's voice shakes.

My jaw relaxes and I lap at her hard nipple with my tongue. Steph rewards me with a buck of her thigh. I moan as I take her breast in my mouth.

"So good," Steph whines. I ride her leg faster, pinch and suck her nipple harder. "So good to mommy. I'm so– so lucky."

Already I start to spill, feeling my eggs clump and roll between my thighs. My tentacles start working, but Steph's pussy is just out of reach. It's a reminder of what she's wanted me to do to her for months, ever since she showed me just how much she loves my tentacles.

I pull back, both of us letting out little noises of disappointment. "Bath," I breathe. "And food. Let's make sure you're nice and ready for me." I reach down and stroke my tentacles.

Steph swallows but nods. "I'll order us… something for dinner."

She gets out of the shower but I linger, cleaning up the mess I started. Once I get out of the shower I start the bath, making sure the water is just the right temperature. In the bedroom Steph is ordering every fish dish off the menu, finishing it off with a lava cake. The bath is halfway full when she struts back into the room, still wet and naked.

"Oh, I should have asked if you wanted anything in particular."

"I like sushi," I tell her. "And smoked salmon, and fish and chips."

She sits on the edge of the bath and touches the water. "Perfect…"

"Not yet," I say. Steph tilts her head. I grab my toiletry bag and pull out two bath bombs. "You can choose lavender or rose."

"Rose," Steph coos as she plucks the bath bomb with dried rose petals out of the bag. She drops it into the tub and we watch it fizz– but we're both impatient.

I get in the bath first, offering Steph a hand. We lower ourselves into the water together, Steph settling into my lap. Water splashes over the lip of the tub. More spills over as I caress Steph's chest. Rose petals dance around us.

She giggles as my thumb flicks at her erect nipples. "I think those are plenty clean, dear."

I move down to her stomach, squeeze her hips before groping her thighs. "I can't help myself," I tell her. *I love your body* I think but decide to show her instead. My lips press against every bit of visible skin. I let my nails drag across her body beneath the water. When Steph shifts her body my tentacles find new places to latch onto and caress. I need more hands. Though judging by Steph's little gasps and moans she's plenty happy.

Finally I let my hand slide between her thighs. Two fingers tease her pussy while my thumb massages that bundle of flesh that makes her whole body shake. My other arm wraps around her stomach, keeping her back pressed against my chest.

I think about the night we watched videos together and fuck her the way she fucks herself: fast and hard. But whenever she lifts her hips I pull my hand back, leaving her empty. "So mean…" she whimpers. Then when she settles my fingers return, pumping just as hard and fast as if they never left. Steph said it herself: I can be rough with her.

As fun as the game is watching her finish is even better. She lifts her hips and I let her ride out her orgasm on my fingers. My teeth gnaw at my lip, trying to distract myself from the bubbling lust between my own legs. When Steph settles my hand rests between her breasts, feeling her heartbeat.

There's a knock at the door. "Wait here," I tell her and kiss the conch of her ear. The air is so cold I want to just dive back into the warm water and nuzzle up to Steph's hot body. Instead I grab a robe from the wall and answer the door. Our food is here. Or I should say our feast. There's about a dozen plates covered with silver tops keeping the food warm.

Back in the room there's not a whole lot of table space. I point at the cart. "Can I just… keep that for a bit?" The bellhop, bless him, nods. I take the cart and push it deep into the room by the coffee table and chairs.

Steph walks out of the bathroom, wearing the other white robe. "Hungry?"

"Not for food." I grab her hips and push her onto the bed. She smiles up at me as I push aside her robe, opening her legs to admire her wet pussy. I drag a lazy finger from her clit down her slick cunt. "I think you're ready."

"Yes," Steph breathes. "Yes, please Lydia. I want it."

She makes this so easy. "Want what?" I start touching myself.

"I want you to breed me. Completely stuff me full till I can't walk– till I can't think of anything other than your tentacles."

"Sounds like that's already all you think about." The air goes from hotel-ice-cold to hot in a snap. There's a tingling around my tentacles I've never felt before. Maybe they're more erogenous than even I realized.

"It's all I want," Steph admits. "Please– fuck me like no one else can."

I get on my knees. Holding Steph's hips I pull her to me, my knees keeping her wide open while her pussy shines like sunlight across waves. Steph sits up, watching with my same interest. I let my tentacles explore her. They're tentative at first, the tips exploring her lips and folds, brushing her clit not aware of what that will do to her.

Steph bites her lip, holding back whimpering moans.

Finally one of the tentacles finds her cunt and dives inside her. "*Oh.*" Steph gasps.

They all flock then to her cunt, some tentacles spreading her open while the rest plunge inside her. I buck my hips. Grab Steph's shoulder and push her down, using her as leverage as I start grinding.

"Oh my God–" Steph cries. "Th-there's so many, fuck– fuck me, *fuck.*" Her hands fly to my ass, groping me and guiding my thrusts. I hold the underside of her thigh to keep her nice and open for me. I pull back, wanting to see her stuffed with tentacles.

I'm already spilling, warmed up from our teasing in the bathroom. My tentacles have started to retreat, grabbing my pearl like eggs and bringing them to Steph.

"Take a breath," I advise Steph as the first egg is pressed inside her. She does as I say, taking slow, deep breaths as more and more eggs are presented to her pussy.

"Lydia…" She whines. "It's so much–"

"We've just started, you can't be full yet." I navigate past the forest of tentacles and press my thumb inside her. She goes stiff, gasping in surprise. "Plenty of room." When I pop my thumb out two tentacles reach for her at once, gifting her eggs.

It's such a beautiful sight. Steph is full of me and somehow taking more and more. There are always a few tentacles inside her, pushing and pulsing. Some of my smaller tentacles are focused on her clit, suctioning themselves to it. Steph is so good, inhaling deep breaths and exhaling with a moan. She grips the sheets but keeps her hips steady.

With my tentacles doing all the work I'm free to stroke her cheek. "Such a good mommy. You've taken so much and haven't spilled even a little bit."

As much as I love watching her be filled I lean down to kiss her. She pulls me to her, grabbing my hair same as she grabbed the sheets. I bite her bottom lip. She groans with pleasure. Her hands are all over my backside. Her perfectly manicured nails dig into my ass, claw at my shoulder blades.

I don't think we've ever been this rough with each other but we're *mating*. That's not really a romantic gesture. It's so much more messy and animalistic. Steph might be Human but the way she scratches at my back and bites my neck makes me think she's more of a monster than I am.

At one point she latches onto my neck, not unlike my tentacles latching to her thighs. First it's just her lips and tongue– then her teeth sink into me. I cry out as she sucks at the bite on my neck. "Steph– Stephanie, God!"

I have to push her away, trying to maintain some control. I expect a smirk on Steph's face. Instead she just pants, tongue exposed and a sheen across her lips. When I study her cunt she's finally starting to spill, her hole full and gaping. I use my fingers to push the eggs up inside her, finding now there's much less room for me to work with.

"Good girl, you're nearly there, almost done." I'm not sure if it's my words or fingers that push her over the edge but her thighs shake and I feel her body tighten. I refuse to relent, pushing deeper inside her. Her mouth is slack and her breathing shallow. Eyes glazed over as they roll back in her head.

My tentacles deflate, recognizing that there is no more space for them to work. I pull out my fingers and several eggs pop out with them. My fingers spread Steph open, letting her leak onto her robe.

Now I'm the one panting. My body is electric as I'm fixated on her spilling cunt.

"How do you feel?" I ask her but I can't tear my eyes away from her pussy.

"It's like… you're still inside me…" She flutters her lashes and with her cheeks and lips so flush she reminds me of a storybook princess. "There's so much…"

"Will you be okay if I grab another towel?" I hate to just leave her like this but I doubt the robe will be enough.

"Yes."

I kiss her forehead before grabbing washcloths, running one of them under hot water and keeping the rest of them dry. On the bed I clean up the mess around her thighs and dripping down her ass. It's a constant effort but far from a chore.

"Relax," I tell her. "Relax for me…"

Steph shuts her eyes, taking slow breaths. I almost think she'll fall asleep still filled with my eggs. But she eventually sits up and watches as her pussy spills my eggs. She fills herself with her fingers. "More," she says under her breath.

I grab her wrist and yank her hand away. "You'll get more,

promise. Now you need to relax." She pouts but I start sucking on her fingers and that fixes her mood.

It takes time, but once there are no more eggs I wipe her down with a wet towel one last time. I kiss her chin. Then her cheeks, her eyes, and finally softly on the lips. Steph rests her head against my chest and I stroke her hair. My heart still thuds like thunder.

Finally I say to her, "Let's eat. Talk for a bit."

We're both slow to leave the bed but once we start poking around the plates our stomachs grumble. I take some haddock, she grabs some fries from the fish and chips. The plate of sushi sits between us. We pick and choose from the plates like it's our personal buffet.

Steph cuts at her tuna while slurping buttered pasta with shrimp. She points with the fork at my neck. "Sorry about that."

I touch my sore neck, my flesh still throbbing. "Don't be. It's like a trophy."

She snorts and grabs a sushi roll with her fingers.

"So, did that live up to your expectations?"

Steph's cheeks are full of food. She responds with an enthusiastic nod before swallowing. "I loved it. Every second. After sex wasn't bad… It was just…"

"Slow. And you're impatient." I spear a potato from her plate.

"I was patient all summer," she points out. "Just laying there for so long got a little tedious."

I nod, not sure how to fix that but glad she's being honest.

"I want to do it again."

"We will."

"Tonight." She insists.

"Tomorrow." I can already see her lips moving and so I press a finger to her mouth. "I love how eager you are, but that was pretty intense for the both of us. Let's just take the rest of the night slow. Besides, I told you I was hungry for something other than food." I press my forehead against hers. "You're the best desert."

"Fine," she huffs past my fingers. When I return to my plate, Steph has an idea. "You can breathe underwater right? We could always get back in the tub."

I tell her yes with a kiss.

CHAPTER
Fourteen

THE SEX ALL BLURS TOGETHER, Steph and I spend our mornings and evenings tangled up in each other. We fuck on the bed and in the bath. Taste each other before breakfast. Fondle each other even as we drift to sleep. It's a wonder we leave the room at all but whenever we're laying there catching our breath I look out over the balcony and find the sea calling to me.

I remember our outings more clearly. The casinos feel like spaceships, not a single window in sight, nevermind clocks or anything to help you keep track of time. I win a dollar in blackjack. Steph shows me how to find conch shells between the rocks. We built a sandcastle together. When the lighthouse opens we visit it and climb to the very top.

The boardwalk is like something out of a movie but not because it's spectacular or awe inspiring. Well, the view of the ocean is beautiful. Waves crashing against the sand as the sky shifts from yellow to orange to pink. On the boardwalk proper, the opposite direction of the natural beauty, I'm met with t-shirt shops, places to buy hermit crabs, and obnoxious flashing arcades and games. It's all so fake like a movie set,

which somehow makes the sun and sea all the more spectacular.

Steph and I hold hands. She wears a beaded swimsuit
cover over a tank top and pair of shorts and I'm dressed the
same but without the cover. As we walk, I point out every
shirt that proclaims a love of MILFs. She rolls her eyes and I
laugh harder and harder each time. Finally she spots one
before I do, snatching my wrists to prevent me from pointing
it out.

She interlaces her fingers with mine. "Win me something?" She nods over to a row of carnival games. They're all
different but boast grand prizes. Plushies hang from their
necks from the walls and ceilings of the booths. Dark. Or
maybe I'm the dark-sided one.

I scope out the games, letting a few patrons go before us.
The water gun game is easy. Deceptively so. I'm sure it has
nothing to do with your actual aim and everything to do with
whichever water gun you pick. There's ring toss and just like
at the country fairs back in Michigan they use milk bottles as
targets. Finally there's darts. It seems like the most fun till I
realize your prize is determined by a piece of paper hidden
inside the balloon. Steph should get to pick her prize.

So ring toss it is. We pay five dollars and I get five rings. I
expect my first toss to be a fluke, a practice round, but I
manage to catch the lip of one of the bottles where the ring
spins before settling.

"Oh!" Steph bounces on her toes like a little kid. "Good
job!"

Spirit of the County Fair, guide my hand I think before
tossing the second ring. It lands and Steph practically shrieks
with excitement.

"I always thought these games were rigged," Steph
admits.

I glance over at the guy running the booth but he's
unfazed by her comment. I'm sure he had much worse

shouted at him. It makes me wonder how people even get these jobs? The County Fair was all farmers and carnies– the same people every single year. It must get tedious hitting up the same small towns.

I wonder if Steph would like the County Fair…

My thoughts are interrupted by none other than Steph herself, rubbing my shoulder in a comforting circular motion. "Two out of five isn't bad."

Well, now I *need* to play a perfect game. It's like Steph can read my mind. She giggles, hiding her lips being her finger-tips as I line up my next shot. The ring flies and lands right around the neck of the bottle. As does the fourth ring.

Steph kisses my cheek.

"I haven't won yet." I hold up the last ring like it's some-thing precious, a pearl I've snagged from the bottom of the ocean. I toss it, a bit overconfident. It hits the side of a bottle then falls to the floor.

The disappointment hits my stomach just as the attendant shows me what prizes I can pick from. I glare at an oversized kraken at the very top of the wall, the five ring prize just out of reach. "Whichever one you like," I grumble. Disappoint-ment churns in my stomach as if a storm is brewing. I swear I'm not a sore loser.

She picks a dolphin with oversized eyelashes. She beams. "It's so cute!" She holds the dolphin up to my face. "It's almost the same shade of blue as you!"

I purse my lips but a laugh bubbles up past my pout. She really is the eye of the storm. Nothing phases her and it makes me want to follow in her path.

We keep walking down the boardwalk, the dolphin under Steph's arm. We pass a group of teenagers, groaning about school starting in a few weeks. Just like that the storm is back, wreaking havoc on my stomach and soul.

I squeeze Steph's hand. "I don't want to ruin our date… We should talk about what comes next."

Steph's eyes are wide and I don't blame her. I shouldn't have mentioned ruining the date. Communication is hard. Less so with Steph. A month ago, at Bistro 11, she was so upfront and confident. It couldn't have been easy to be so vulnerable, to ask if I would be open to her arrangement. Now it's my turn.

"I know you're going to be busy when summer ends. Me too. So, we'll see each other less." I run a finger across her knuckle.

"I'm okay with that," Steph says. "It's like you said, we'll both be busy, and I knew that from the start. I almost told you that this could only be for the summer."

"Why didn't you?"

She looks up at me, her dark eyes catch the yellow-orange sky making her eyes appear gold. "Wishful thinking." She laughs. "Summers are so short. I wanted more than a few months."

"I want that too," I tell her. "I still– I'm okay with seeing you less. But still seeing you."

"Less is vague, Guppy." She's smiling though her voice is sad. "Will we see each other once a month? Once a fiscal quarter?"

"Whenever works?" I offer. "I'm sure we can find a week-end. Grab lunch together?"

Steph licks her lips. "I don't want you to get lonely."

I let out a dry chuckle. "I won't," I promise her.

She doesn't believe me. "I know I was hesitant at the start about us being open, but–"

I stop dead in my tracks. "I could never do that to you. Not after what Roman did."

"You deserve all the attention," Step says. "Really Lydia. I'd hate it if you missed out on a chance at love, at a life with someone, because of me."

It's like she's just poured a cup of ice water over my head. Which isn't fair to her. I never wanted to find love. I'm not looking for forever right now. How can I just choose *someone* to be my future? I've felt this way for years but never been able to articulate it.

Dark blue begins to drown out the pastel sky. The lights of the boardwalk are even brighter now, the neon intoxicating. There's a ferris wheel that has been looming over us for some time, but I look at it like it's just poofed into existence.

"Are you afraid of heights?" I ask her.

Steph shakes her head. "I'd love to see the view."

We get in line and despite the ferris wheel spinning oh so slowly, the line moves fast. I'm running out of time, even if in reality, Steph and I will still go back to the same hotel room and ride in the same car tomorrow. I'll still have her number and she'll still have mine. We don't have to pretend like this summer was a fluke.

"To be honest Steph, I don't have it in me to find someone else."

"Some people are lucky," she responds with ease. "I've got friends who met their partners on the subway. Met the love of their lives because a flight got canceled. You can't *know*, Lydia."

I wish she'd call me Guppy.

"Okay, so say that does happen, I find true love in central park or lock eyes with some pretty girl at graduation– we wouldn't start dating immediately."

Steph tilts her head to the side like she's never considered this.

"I would tell you. I would *want* to tell you. You're more invested in my love life than I am. I could tell you there's someone and we can do our goodbyes then. If that ever happens."

Just like that we're at the front of the line. A pair of teens get out of the cart and Steph and I climb in right after them.

I think there's an awkwardness in the air but Steph blurts out, "I know you said girls your age can't compare to me, and

I appreciate and believe you but it's still easy to imagine you falling for someone else."

"Because I'm irresistible." I say, waiting for her cheeks to get a little flush before adding, "to you." I kiss her temple.

Steph whines. "I just know there's pretty girls in New York."

"Yeah, she's named Stephanie."

Steph looks out over the coastline. I also turn, looking out over the island, catching sight of the lighthouse, the casinos, and the houses of the people who simply *live* here. This place has been a fantasy, it's easy to forget that the salty air is just an everyday thing to so many people. In time, will Steph be less of a fantasy? I can't imagine getting bored of this. Not the vacation, not the luxury hotels and big dinners. I mean this, sitting here next to her without a care for anyone else.

Except that means facing reality.

"I don't think I want to get married," I tell her. "Ever. To anyone."

"Why?" She asks without judgment. It's just the natural follow up to a statement like that.

"I don't know," I admit. "My parents are together and happy. I know it does work. But the title of wife doesn't excite me. I don't dream of being called someone's wife or introducing someone as my wife." I rest my chin on the ferris wheel cart railing. "Maybe I'm just a coldhearted bitch."

"Well you're neither of those things," Steph says. "You know yourself, that's what I've always admired about you." She rests her head on my shoulder as we reach the summit. The ferris wheel stops right at the top, the sea breeze catching our hair. "I'd hate to see you try and be something you aren't. To miss out on the parts of you that are a little more rough, scaly even."

"So that's not a deal breaker? That I'm never going to get down on one knee?"

"I've already been married once," she reminds me. "Can't say I'm dying to do it all over again."

Relief floods my body. I could float right down from the top of this ride, the two of us hand-in-hand, unburdened by an expectation neither of us want. "So you're okay with us being casual. Committed, but casual."

"I wasn't sure at first but, yes. I would be happy with that. I just want to keep seeing you."

Back at the hotel I step out onto the balcony, close my eyes, and listen to ocean waves crash against the sand. Try to ignore how much my chest hurts. It's our last night. Everything is still in my grasp and yet the emptiness is already starting to set in. I tell myself it's okay to miss her even if she's just a few feet away. Saying goodbye to summer is never easy.

Inside, Steph is asleep in bed. I whisper in her ear, "Let's do this again next summer."

———

"YOU WANT one last ride in the sports car?" Steph asks as we dive north up the highway.

I think about it, deciding I'll get a little more time with Steph if we stop at her house before she drops me off at the apartment for the last time. "Sure. But I get to pick the music."

"Oh, excellent." She giggles. Her face is so bright. She got a bit of a tan from our hours on the beach and her hair is still windswept. The sadness I felt on the balcony is still here, and it makes me want to take a photo of her like this. Some tangible thing to remind myself of this weekend. Even if the hickies on my neck are proof enough, proof that's still a bit sore.

"How are you going to explain your bruises to your roommates?" She asks like she's reading my mind.

"I might just tell them."

She takes her eyes off the road. "Really? About us?"

"They already know I have a friend I've been seeing. I'll just tell them that friend is… a little more than a friend."

"Your business partner." She laughs, returning her attention to the road. "You should tell them. It's not good, keeping secrets."

"Sure isn't."

We pull into Steph's driveway only to see there's a car already parked, a nice looking red sedan. The second Steph puts her SUV in park, Roman exits the drivers side.

Before I can react Steph unbuckles her seatbelt. "Stay here." She gets out, leaving the car on.

I sink in my seat, hoping the dashboard will hide me. I think about just curling into a ball and hiding under the seat. Accepting this is my life and moving into Steph's car. At least then I wouldn't have to say goodbye to Steph or tell my roommates that actually this whole summer I've been fucking the MILF from the pool and having her buy me jewelry instead of helping pay for groceries. Though there is a bottle of tequila on top of the fridge courtesy of Steph's bank account. That's one bullet dodged.

Even from inside the car I can hear them bickering. Roman insists he was supposed to drop the kids off at 12:30 and it's one now. Steph doesn't understand why he's upset about an extra half hour with the kids. It's the principal. It's him being an ass. Don't curse in front of the kids– but it's a bit late for that when they're already arguing.

I pop my head over the dashboard and spot Steven doing the same thing from the backseat. He unbuckled his seatbelt and turned around, looking at me from the back window. He waves at me with a toothless smile.

The car is still on. I could drive away– drive back to the shore and just disappear into the ocean. Grand theft auto feels like a petty crime compared to this shit-show.

"At least tell me where you've been?" Roman demands.

"We went to the shore, happy?"

"So you're taking her on vacations now?"

The air is blasting but I still feel like I'm suffocating in here. I grab my phone and click Jess as a contact.

> SOS can you come to Oasis?

> Huh? I thought you were on vacation. Why are you at work?

> I'll tell you about it when you pick me up.

> Alright fine. I'm on my way.

I grab my bag from the backseat and exit the car. Without even looking at Steph or Roman I walk down the driveway.

"Where do you think you're going?" Roman's voice is like nails on a chalkboard. He catches up to me and though it would be easy enough to walk around him, I let him stop me. I cross my arms, lean back on my heels like I have nothing to hide. The hickey on my neck burns and it's like he can sense it.

His eyes go wide as he looks at my neck. He laughs, a strained, awkward sound. "Are you serious? Walking away after–" He touches his own neck. "I don't even want to *know* what you two have been doing."

"Good because it's none of your business." I scowl.

"I have a right to know what's happening in my house."

"Not your house." I point out.

He crosses his arms. "How would you know?"

God he's such a baby.

Steph walks over and touches Roman's shoulder. "This is between us. Lydia I'm so sorry–"

"It's fine," I shake my head. "My roommate is picking me up."

Steph's face falls. It's hard to believe just half an hour ago she looked so giddy, like a new woman. It's like looking at her for the first time. She's beautiful, so fucking sexy, but there's an exhaustion behind her eyes.

I walk around Roman and leave. It takes about twenty minutes to walk from Steph's house to Oasis. When I get there, Jess is sitting in her car checking her phone. I pull out my own phone, forgetting I have it silenced. She texted me a few times asking where I am. I just walk up to the car and get into the passenger's side.

"Shit!" Jess jumps. "Where did you–" She stops mid-thought.

I don't think I'm crying but Jess' reaction makes me think otherwise. I touch my cheeks, finding they're dry.

Jess pulls out of the parking lot. We don't speak the whole drive back to the apartment. I don't feel sad, or guilty even though I probably should. I barely feel the seat beneath me. When I close my eyes it's like I'm out at sea in the depths of the ocean. Floating and at the mercy of the current with no idea which way is up to the surface or down to the inky depths.

I don't even notice we're parked and back home till Jess says my name. Judging from her tone she's said it a couple times. "Lydia!"

"Thanks for picking me up." I get out of the car, proud of my legs for keeping me upright.

CHAPTER
Fifteen

I'm sorry it's taken me so long to text things were crazy here.

Don't apologize I know it's not been great.

What did you tell him?

That it's none of his business what I do with my free time. He wants to talk to our lawyers.

He's just throwing a fit because he can.

Fuck I'm so sorry, Steph.

Not to sound like a broken record but don't.

We did nothing wrong. I already know he's going to argue from the money angle and say I'm irresponsible. Maybe make it seem like I'm an inattentive mother.

I know you're not those things, but will a judge?

I'm sure it won't get that far. Our lawyers will work it out, don't worry.

I am worried.

Steph, your kids are your world. I don't want to threaten that.

Maybe till the lawyers work things out we take a break.

Is that what you want?

It's not about what I want. I can't fuck up your life like this.

I care too much about you, Steph.

JESSIE AND GOLDIE stand on either side of my horizontal body. I'm flat on my back, on the floor, the bottle of tequila my companion.

"So… how's the floor rotting treating you?" Jess asks in a gentle voice.

"This is savasana yoga," I grab the bottle by the neck, "Actually."

Goldie rolls her eyes, her feathery arms crossed. "Let's just leave her alone, Jess. She's clearly got it under control."

With the cap off the bottle I open my mouth and waterfall a shot worth of liquor.

"She's barely packed and she's moving out in three days!"

"She owns like, ten things."

Goldie is wrong. I have a lot more shit now thanks to Steph. Suits, shoes, jewelry, a leather duffle bag, new sunglasses… but maybe it's best I just leave them here. Let Jess and Goldie split them. Jess would look nice in those aviators and my gold hoops match Goldie's wings perfectly.

It'll be like this summer never happened.

Jess scowls. "If anyone can help her get out of this funk it's you."

"Because I've had my heart broken by a girl before?" Goldie's tone is so sharp it makes me sit up.

My head spins from the blood rush. "Don't fight." I hang my still spinning head in my hands. "Please."

Goldie and Jess are silent.

"We're ordering take out," Jess says finally but there's still tension in her voice. "What do you want?"

"Beef and broccoli."

I reach for the bottle again but Goldie snatches it. "I think you've had enough of the *communal* tequila."

I pout, muttering, "I bought it." But I did get it for the three of us.

Jess and Goldie go to the kitchen and make themselves to-go cups of tequila and random chasers we have in the kitchen. Jess takes a sip, smacking her lips. "Not bad. We're walking to get the food so it'll be a while."

I acknowledge them with a wave and they leave. Even with the lights on the apartment feels so dark. I stand up and open the curtains to the sliding door onto our deck. The sun is setting and the sky is sherbet colors. The deck is basically Goldie's room so I've spent very little time out on it. Better late than never.

The whole balcony is as wide as my wingspan. Most of it is taken up by Goldie's nest made of cloth and gold wire. I rest my chin in the railing looking out over town. Before moving out east I would have considered this place a city; tall buildings, traffic jams, more than three restaurants– that's what cities were to me. Everything my tiny town doesn't have.

Naive. I'm so fucking naive.

My phone buzzes and I grab it from my sweatshirt pocket, expecting a text from Jess saying they can't make my order or something. Instead Steph's name pops up.

> I can't send this all in one text so stand by.

She's left me on read for weeks. Which is fine. It's what we needed– what I needed. Just let the relationship drown like a drunk businessman in the country club pool. Except I can't stop staring at the three little dots telling me she's typing. The wall of text makes me jump before I read it.

> You're right. You're always so right. My kids are what I care about most, more than my job, more than a summer fling. Whatever Roman throws at me I am willing to fight tooth and nail to keep my kids. Typical momma bear. Things will work out. Don't blame yourself for what happened. I wish I could say that's my only request but you know me, I'm a bit needy that way.

It takes a minute but a second text comes through.

> Lydia you're amazing, so, so amazing.
> Confident and cool and smart and sexy. I
> know you're so much more than that though.
> I wish we'd had more time and I could have
> seen more parts of you, even the less
> impressive parts. I hope you know that's
> always what I wanted most, to see you
> completely. I wanted to watch you and
> support you, always.
>
> Truthfully I wasn't sure how to do that. Be
> there for you but also have distance. I know
> I'm not ready to enter a standard relationship
> right now. Whenever I saw you, I just wanted
> to give you everything. So I came up with our
> arrangement. I don't regret it. Maybe that's
> silly but I don't regret a single moment.
>
> So now the requests. You let me know when
> you're looking for an internship. I can put in a
> good word pretty much anywhere. I can tell
> you who's looking for people, they never let
> the public know about their best positions. I
> still want to do that for you because I know
> you'd be a great asset to any company who
> hires you.
>
> Second request, and remember this is a
> request. If you could leave space for me in
> your heart. I don't know when Lydia, but I
> promise you someday we can be together
> like before. I know the longer I make you wait
> the less likely you'll need me. You deserve to
> fall in love and start a life with someone. I
> know you don't want the white picket fence
> but maybe an apartment in SoHo with a girl?
> It's selfish but I want that girl to be me.

> I know this is a lot over text but is email any better? Just to recap: Don't blame yourself. Let me know when you need a job. And if it's possible you could love an old lady like me (remember I'm only getting older) I would do anything for the chance to prove myself to you. Again, and again, and again.

A drop of water splashes against my phone screen. I blink and two more *plop* across the screen. When was the last time I cried? When Ari broke up with me? No, it was that stupid internship. I wasted my tears on *that?* Since then apathy has been my only counselor. And she's kind of shit at it.

Cars honk below and I study the streets searching for Goldie and Jess. I think I know how I want to respond, but food first. Maybe a bath too. Steph says these are just requests but I'm a woman of my word. I want to make sure I don't leave her hanging.

Jess and Goldie finish the bottle of tequila together over dinner. Watching them wrap their arms around each other, press their noses to each other's hair, and giggle like school girls makes me jealous. Who cares what you call your relationship so long as you're both happy? Those two might not have figured it out yet but they will.

"We'll stay in touch, right?" I ask them as I bring everyone's dishes to the sink.

Goldie, the less drunk of the two, nods. "New York isn't far."

"Come visit us!" Jess slurs with excitement. "Rutgers parties are sooooo much more fun! Like does NYU even have frat houses? We'll getcha in." Jess giggles like she's already pulled off her perfect plan. Goldie giggles with her.

I give the two of them some privacy and go to my room. It looks the same as it has all summer. I'm going to have to really focus on packing tomorrow. Love Jess and Goldie but I don't want them using my good bath stuff. I'm going to need a lot of long baths in my final semester.

As I run myself a bath I stare at my phone screen. The thing isn't even on, my brooding reflection getting worse and worse by the second. I tap the screen as if I'm typing out the message, reading it in my head. Maybe I should look back at Steph's text but honestly, it's like I've memorized them: *Don't blame yourself. You'd be a great asset to any company who hires you. Leave room in your heart for me.*

I open my texts and send my grand gesture.

Okay.

<3

Epilogue

ALFIE TOSSES A STAPLED copy of spreadsheets across the conference table. "Fuck me I can't look at these numbers again." The cityscape behind him is a gray haze, summer long gone and dreary New York winter days ahead.

I tap a capped highlighter against my own packet. "They might be different this time." We've been working on this project for a week with no forward movement but there have been several meetings. We have several more next week to talk about this very spreadsheet.

Alfie loosens his tie. His real name is Albert Thomas Jefferson III but everyone calls him Alfie. Including the hedge manager who golfs with his dad on the weekends. "Are you seriously going to look through the whole spreadsheet again?"

"It's seriously my job, so, yes." I highlight a section just too fuck with him. He's right, the numbers haven't changed far as I can tell. At this point it's like a hunt for buried treasure, looking for that elusive decimal point that will fix everything. If it exists.

Alfie slumps in his chair like the big boy he is. "New necklace?" He gestures across his loose collar. "That Van Cleef?"

I look up from my paper. "You noticed?" I absentmindedly touch the mother of pearl Alhambra pendant.

"Yeah, it's the kind of shit my mom wears."

"She has good taste." I wait, just long enough for him to put his guard down. "She single?"

"Nice," he snorts. "Real nice, Lydia." He gets up, not bothering to push in his rolling chair. "Well, I'm bailing. Have fun with that."

I check my watch. It's 4:30, on a Friday, sure, but still thirty minutes before we're supposed to leave. I thought Triton interns would be more hungry, that they'd frenzy over the most meaningless task like sharks in chum filled water. Turns out I'm the only shark in the water while everyone else is just a barnacle attached to their parent's bank accounts.

As I flip through the spreadsheet again I wonder if Alfie has a point. Except it was my 'tenacity and conscientious energy with every project' that got me this spot. Program manager's words, not mine.

My senior fall semester I focused on finding a winter internship and frankly, I got lucky. Or I should say Mr. Greysea was right and people back out of his company's internships all the time.

Getting my last college credits while also being a full time intern was impossible on paper. NYU was nice enough to let me walk at graduation even though I had to take a summer course for my last credit. My parents flew out and everything. They were smiling so hard they never asked how much the summer semester costs. For a day, I forgot all about it. A day of bliss without student loans or rent payments.

Which gave me time to call Jess and ask if I was a decent enough roommate she'd let me live with her and Goldie again. The train sucks but New York City rent is so much worse. All and all it's worked out. Not that I can take all the credit.

I grab my phone. 4:45 on a Friday and I don't have any plans. Which is an easy fix.

> Drinks? I want to check out that speakeasy on 47th

In the heart of the theater district?

> You'll live. Or do I need to convince you?

A little convincing wouldn't hurt.

> Well there's the ambiance and I've never been to a speakeasy before. We can be obvious there. Maybe I'll have you buy a round for the whole bar. We can stay till the last train to Jersey and pretend it's just the two of us in our train car.

> Also I'm asking and you can't say no <3

You've convinced me <3

The last fifteen minutes fly by, maybe because I start packing up early and stop by the bathroom to adjust my hair. It's 5:01 when I step out onto the sidewalk and head north to 47th street. I'm not the only one. Every restaurant and bar I pass boasts a happy hour and people pour in. I'm a little worried I won't be able to spot Steph in the crowd.

But of course I see her. Dressed in a skirt and smart suit coat, her dark hair pulled back to show off her round cheeks. She spots me and walks toward me and I have to stop myself from running to meet her. Despite the build up, we're both casual.

"Hi," I say.

"Hello," she smiles, then points to a nearby door. "This the place?"

"I'm not sure," I admit.

Inside is a room with several book cases. Steph pouts. "I hate puzzles."

I snort and start rifling through the books, tilting the spines back. "You've got to work for your old fashioned."

"Or I could just let a strong, sexy Guppy do it for me."

"Start looking, babe."

Steph huffs but follows my lead, examining the bookshelves. We're both so focused we don't realize we're inching closer and closer to each other till our hands settle on the same book. Her nails are still the same pink as last summer. She starts to pull her hand away but I grab it, bring it to my lips and kiss her fingertips.

"Was this your game all along?"

I respond by kissing her palm.

I still don't know what to call us. Girlfriends, friends with benefits, sugar baby and momma, Steph insists we're business partners. It's occurred to me more than once that out in the ocean, pods don't need names for what we are. I think anyone whose seen us in passing, in dim lit bars and five star restaurants can tell that we care for each other. That my heart races whenever she's near, that her bright smiles are for me and me alone.

All I know for certain is I love her. I don't need anything else.

Steph giggles as I kiss wet and loud smooches across her palm. The wall creeks and we jump back. The bookcase slides open, a few people exiting through the newfound doorway. Steph and I look at each other before slipping past them to enter the bar.

"We *so* cheated," Steph comments.

"Life isn't always fair," I point out. "Gotta roll with the wins as they come."

Finally we hold hands and take a seat at the bar, our knees touching. I let Steph pick out our drinks. We chat about work, or I should say complain. I tell her my parents want me to visit for Christmas and that I've never gone home for the holidays. I've never told her that. We're still learning things about each other.

I hope we learn things about ourselves and each other for a long time.

Acknowledgments

Oh wow this novella was a doozie.

First thank you to Dae Storm who organized and edited *Sapphic Blooms*. Lydia and Steph were born out of that anthology and I will always be grateful.

To Em who was such a cheerleader for this novella. Every beta comment raving about how hot Steph was kept me going. I feel so lucky to call you a friend and mentor.

My beta readers- Morgan, Arson, Lita, and Wendy, who notice all the things I missed and made me smile with their comments. Seriously this wouldn't exist if you hadn't taken the time and care to read it, so thank you.

Sophie, my cover artist, who always understands my brain and makes the juiciest cover art. My life's goal is to create as many gay monster things as possible so we can keep collaborating.

Wendy again, who surprised me with fan art while I was deep in edits. I might be a writer, but there are no words for the joy I still feel looking at your art.

To the Cozy Corner, who helped me when I was stuck and reminded me that PH is important to fish.

Thank you to Chappell Roan and her album *The Rise and Fall of a Midwest Princess* which was a huge inspiration for this story. Special shout out to the track Naked in Manhattan, the official *Mother of Pearl* track.

And as always to my partner, Bear. Who is deeply afraid of the ocean. But loves me, a fishfucker, anyway.

About the Author

Arin was born and raised along the American east coast and has called the city, the shore, and the country their home. They've come a long way from writing anime fanfiction in their bedroom and even have a BA in creative writing. When they're not writing, Arin enjoys playing tabletop games, drinking coffee, and collecting bits and bobbles. They currently live with their partner, cat, and lizard.

www.ingramcontent.com/pod-product-compliance
Lightning Source LLC
Chambersburg PA
CBHW071513140726
47997CB00005B/1956